T0064006

Love
Unconditionally
and LIVE
Joyfully

Love
Unconditionally
and LIVE
Joyfully

Qamruddin

PARTRIDGE

A Penguin Random House Company

To order additional copies of this book, contact
Partridge India
000 800 10062 62
orders.india@partridgepublishing.com

www.partridgepublishing.com/india

Words from Author of the Book

We are desperately in need of hope, enjoyment, contentment, courage, serenity, faith, peace of mind and gratitude for Almighty. To cater to that need, it has been an abundant pleasure to write this book. It will be even a greater pleasure to observe that it will be received in the same spirit, in which it has been written.

We are all busy and galloping ahead in frenzy most of the time, but there comes the quiet hour, when we must sit still and take stock of our life. There is a need to relax, pause and ponder.

I have weaved together motivational success principles in story form in this book to inspire you in day-to-day life. It is going to make an interesting reading and at the same time it will give you enough food for thought.

It is up to you whether you categorize this book, 'Love Unconditionally and Live Joyfully' either as a fiction or a motivational book, but for me it is both. It is a motivational fiction as my earlier book, 'Love, Live and Leap Ahead'. This book, 'Love Unconditionally and Live Joyfully' will tell you how to put the noble ideology into practice in day-to-day mundane life.

I have intertwined the ideas in the story form in this book to generate curiosity. This is an amazing fiction, incorporating principles of success, happiness, joy and human spirituality and built on insights into unconditional love, forgiveness, gratitude, understanding, enthusiasm, hope and faith. This book is precisely and incisively written, with an unfailing strain of wit, joy and unconditional love running through these lines.

This motivational fiction demonstrates, how you can love unconditionally, live blissfully and be serene and successful in all the circumstances. This is a practical journey into your subconscious mind. Just read it for the joy of reading and let the subconscious take over and ingrain success principles and inspirational ideas into your disposition.

About the Author

Mr. Qamruddin is an experienced and successful motivational trainer, author, life coach, speaker and a compere. He has trained so many persons to live an effective, peaceful and meaningful life.

He worked as Superintendent Customs, Central Excise and Service Tax in the Department of Revenue, Ministry of Finance India. He remained posted in important prestigious organizations like DRI (Directorate of Revenue Intelligence), Delhi; Air Customs, Bombay and Air Customs, Delhi. He got an opportunity to interact with persons from different countries and different walks of life.

He is a renowned sports man and an international Table Tennis player. He represented India and visited Manchester to participate in 9th World Veteran Table Tennis Championship, held at Manchester, England in 1998.

He delves deep into lives and spirits of distinguished thinkers and achievers. He is an adroit storyteller and has already authored five more books; four motivational non-fictions and one more motivational fiction. These books have effectively changed lives of so many persons.

Acknowledgement

First and foremost, I am thankful to you, dear readers. Without your love for my writings, my efforts would have become useless. I would like to be grateful towards you for investing your hard earned money, effort and precious time on this book. I want to be loved unconditionally, not admired by you, as love is lasting and admiration is ephemeral.

I am thankful to my critics and opponents also, without whom I would not have discovered various aspects of life. They helped me examine problems from different angles, face challenges, and find the solutions. They also improved my writing skills.

I am thankful to my family members for faith, love, support, patience and encouragement. I would also like to thank Khadija, my wife; Hafiza, my mother; Farzana, my daughter-in-law; Sheetal, my daughter-in-law for creating an environment, in which I could let my creative juices flow. My family members continue to support me in all my ventures. They always helped me with their time and various practical ideas.

I, especially, thank my elder son, Mohammed Shaz Qamar, himself a great writer of his famous book, 'You Look Fit'. He, along with Farzana, his wife, has helped me with so many practical ideas and time. They inspired to me to keep going, when going was tough.

Mohammed Shiraz Qamar, my younger son, himself a great writer of a famous book, 'Mind Your Intellect', along with his wife, Sheetal has given his valuable time, suggestions and ideas to complete this book. He constantly reviews all my writings, recordings and works. He has been a great inspiration to me for writing this and a few more other books. He has helped me in editing this book, and giving this book a presentable shape.

I am, especially, thankful to Meetakshi for her contribution. She has given plenty of time to review and edit this book. Her perspicacious analysis and guidance helped me improve the presentation style, flow and pattern of this book 'Love Unconditionally and Live Joyfully'.

I am thankful to my publisher and all those who have been connected with me in this endeavor. I am thankful to my friends and colleagues who have been constant source of inspiration to me in this venture and they have given maximum support, time and motivation for completing this book.

Chapter-1

Reena was comfortably ensconced in a sofa chair. No one else was there in the restaurant at this time. Today she was feeling relaxed and free after a hectic shooting for a famous deodorant. She was a self-motivated and an enthusiastic lady, with a positive mental attitude and she could easily motivate herself when tedium started to creeping in. Most of the time, she was joyful and knew how to live a splendid life.

She was a student of psychology, when she decided to join modeling for earning money to look after herself and family. Her gorgeous features, well sculpted body, her pursuit of perfection that was unarguably religious in its fervor. Incessant devotion to her work helped her rise to the acme of glory. With painstaking discipline for working smart, she could learn in a short time, which academies would not have taught her in years. Now she was getting important roles in various popular serials also. Reena had a feeling of an abundance most of time, but she, sometimes, realized that something is missing in her life.

She realized that there was a need for an attitudinal readjustment, if she had to live a truly happy and successful life. She once discussed about her personality deficiency with her close friends Mitali. Mitali was fond of motivational literature and she had attended a few motivational workshops earlier at Bombay. It was difficult to spare time from her busy schedule; still she managed, somehow to attend such workshops. Mitali told her that she got tremendous moral boost after attending such workshops. Mitali had advised Reena also to attend a few of such workshops.

She had received a telephone call yesterday from Mitali, intimating her that a motivational workshop was being organized in an island resort, around fifty Kilometers from the beach. Reena was enormously happy that she could easily attend the workshop and fulfill her cherished desire, that too with her friend Mitali.

She decided to attend the workshop and accordingly telephoned Mitali and chirped with jubilation, "Hi darling… Thanks for your lovely suggestion to attend workshop… Now I have decided to attend it."

"Oh fantastic! I am ecstatic to hear it," squeaked Mitali exultantly. She gave an expressive chuckle, as she was too stunned to hide her happiness. "We are going to have wonderful time together. We have not met for a long time. This is a magnificent opportunity for both of us to spend a few days together."

"Really long time. Millions of cusecs of water might have gone down the Ganges since we met last… What I have to do to participate?" asked Reena.

"Nothing sweetie… Just relax and get ready to reach there tomorrow. I will talk to Vikas and make all the arrangements."

"Thanks," mumbled Reena with joy. "Who is Vikas?"

"He is the main person, the organizer of the workshop, an amazing trainer and a terrific personality. I have earlier attended his workshops," said Mitali with appreciation. "Try to spend maximum time with him. He is a great company and every word he utters is motivational."

"Okay dear, Thank you very much."

"A Boat will pick you up to transport you to the resort," added Mitali after a pause. "They have got their own boat and pickup service."

"Thanks Mitali... You are so sweet... Love you."

"I love you too, my dear."

~~~~~~~

It was a wonderful experience to sail to the island resort. Cold breeze was blowing and caressing her cheeks. Sounds of waves and breeze blended with the sound of boat engine to create a peculiar thrilling sensation. The hilly island was now visible from distance, as the bright sunlight falling on it made it glow. She turned her glance on the side of the boat hearing a splash. She was pleasantly surprised to notice a pair of dolphins jumping joyfully in the air. She had never seen such a view earlier in her life. She looked consistently in the same direction, till she saw them again.

Mitali was already waiting for her near the entrance. Both hugged each other with a tight embrace. Reena was extremely delighted to get such a wonderful greeting, such a welcome and such an overjoyed exclamation from Mitali.

"Welcome my sweetie. We are meeting after ages, after a very long gap," Reena cooed to prattle in cheery rendezvous with boisterous euphoria.

"Yes dear, I am thrilled to meet you here darling. I missed you a lot," Mitali chuckled excitedly and hugged her again. "I am so thrilled. It is wonderful opportunity to be here together."

"Yes, dear."

"How was the journey?" asked Mitali. "You might be tired. May I accompany you to your suite?"

"It was a pleasant journey and enjoyed a lot," cooed Reena. "I will manage it, thanks. Just tell me the suite number."

"Okay; you may go to your suite and get fresh. We will meet after an hour or so on lunch. Your suite no. is 5. Attendant is here and he will take you to your suite," said Mitali motioning at the attendant.

"Thank you very much," said Reena. "I will be back soon, after I get fresh."

"An excellent lunch is waiting for you. They have arranged sea food buffet today," said Mitali. "We will have our lunch together."

"Wow… how wonderful! I love sea food… you very well know," Reena quipped elatedly and sauntered towards her suite. "See you soon, Mitali."

She reached her suite, relaxed in the bath tub and enjoyed shower. She took a cup of tea and relaxed in the bed. She felt fresh after taking a short nap.

When she reached the restaurant, Mitali was already there. She was engrossed in conversation and appeared very happy in the company of a gentleman. She put her hand softly on her shoulder from behind. She turned around and hugged her.

"Come Reena, let us sit down," Mitali prattled with a smile. "Meet Mr. Vikas, a magnificent personality. I am his fan. I never miss an opportunity to attend his workshops. He has changed my life and my attitude."

"I am glad to meet you, Vikas," Reena mumbled with a huge smile spread across her face. She extended her hand for a lively hand shake.

"Mitali often talks about you. You both appear to be close friends."

"Yes Vikas, she is my closest friend. We often spend time together and we have many common and pleasant memories," murmured Reena joyously with her usual lovely smile. "Her very presence makes my life fabulous."

"I am very glad to meet you both gorgeous young ladies," Vikas squeaked with a lovely smile. "We are going to have wonderful time together during our stay here."

"Obviously, we are certainly going to have awesome time here… especially when we have an excellent trainer like you, Vikas. Why have you decided to make all of us stay in the same complex?" asked Mitali. Her eyes lit up with an expression of acute curiosity.

"This is an exceptional workshop in many ways. Firstly, only a small number of persons are going to participate in it. It is going to be a close knit group of 6-8 persons. Secondly, it is being organized in an exotic and exquisite location, far from city life. Thirdly, while staying together, we are going interact more, learn more and practice more," Vikas elaborated. "We all have read good books and have wonderful ideas. We have to engrain these ideas into our subconscious through repeated use, to be effective. Efficacy of these exquisite ideas is more pronounced when we practice them in our day-to-day life and transplant these ideas into others mind," explained Vikas with a smile. "This is the only resort on this exquisite island. I have booked full resort for this workshop."

"Wow, this time it is going to be even more interesting," cooed Mitali joyfully. "We are going to have terrific time here."

"Yes, indeed," Vikas said reassuringly. "It is going to be memorable lifetime experience."

"What about timings and venue for the workshop?" asked Reena interestedly.

"09.00 Hrs. to 17.00 Hrs. will be general timings for the workshop. The workshop will be stretched to 5 days. 20.00 Hrs. to 22.00 Hrs. will be additional time for a few days. There will be tea, lunch and dinner breaks as usual. We are going to stay here together for 7 days. There will be workshop for 5 days and 2 days will be free. You can spend these 2 days the way you like. You may visit beautiful spots on this island, alone or with friends."

"Wonderful!" Reena exclaimed with delight. "Can we visit some nearby places in the evenings also?"

"Of course, Reena. We will have sufficient time to utilize the way we like. We can also easily readjust timings, if there is such a situation. This time we are not adhering to strict time schedule. You all will have 2 full days and a few evenings free, at your disposal. You may swim, dance, paint, read, talk, walk, get massage or simply relax in your suites," Vikas expatiated. "This is a very big island with hills and verdant forests. You may also go on a long drive to these jungles and hilly areas in a group of two or more. You can go for horse riding also."

"What about venue of workshop?"

"This time venue will be different for different days to avoid monotony," said Vikas with a charming smile. "We have already chosen different exotic locations for different days."

"Wow, fantastic," mumbled Mitali. "I will love it."

"You have made beautiful arrangements and seem to have spent lot of money," mumbled Reena with concern.

"You all have contributed huge amounts of money this time. You must get your money's worth," said Vikas. "Shams and Sofia are coming here. They are both Managers in this resort and they are playing significant roles in making elaborate arrangements here at different locations. Both are trying to formally join this workshop, if their General Manager agrees."

"Hi, Vikas. How are you?" Shams prattled cheerfully with a smile. "Meet my colleague, Sofia. We are both going to participate in the workshop. GM has acceded to our request."

"Wow… That is marvelous…Welcome… I am glad to hear that," articulated Vikas with delight. "Meet Reena and Mitali."

"I am delighted to meet you both," shams chuckled and all shook hands.

"Welcome to this beautiful resort," interjected Sofia jubilantly with a lovely smile. "You will get an excellent service. We have properly delegated arrangements to suitable persons," articulated Sofia with a charming smile. There was a glow on her face. She appeared to be joyful and enthusiastic to participate in the workshop. "We are also there to supervise, if there is a need."

"Lunch is ready. Will you like service here on table or opt for buffet?" asked Shams with smile. "Today's specialty is sea food. I hope you all like sea food."

"Yes, I like sea food," murmured Reena. All nodded 'yes' in unison.

"Today we have 6 varieties of sea food to relish, Reena," Sofia quipped with an enticing smile.

"Let us go for buffet. You have arranged wonderful buffet, Shams and Sofia," mumbled Vikas with a smile.

Everybody winded their way through the maze of gastronomic delights. Food was luscious and delicious. Everybody liked the variety, aroma and taste of delectable food.

Chapter-2

Reena was still in a dreamy state when she woke up, hearing, seemingly, orchestrated chirping of birds. After many sleepless nights, last night's sleep was quite refreshing and it rejuvenated her. She was feeling relaxed, blissful and full of energy. She got up and opened the windows. Cold breeze entered and further elevated her blissful mood. There was lot of greenery in the lawn and bushes were replete with colorful flowers. Vikas was already there and walking in the lawn. She was also tempted to go out and smell the fragrant flowers.

"Good morning, Vikas." squeaked Reena. "How are you?"

"I am happy," Vikas quipped. "How was the sleep, Reena?"

"It was superb. I feel relaxed, joyful and delighted."

"There is steam bath facility and a big swimming pool in this resort. Get fresh, go and enjoy these facilities also, if you like."

"Thanks Vikas for letting me know. I will like to go and enjoy," chuckled Reena with a charming smile.

"We will take breakfast together."

"Yes Vikas, Thank you." croaked Reena. "I will be there in time."

Acting on the suggestion, she went to the well-maintained gorgeous pool and had a wonderful swimming. It was a glorious experience to swim in a big swimming pool in a natural setting. She was extremely happy and continued swimming for a long time. She basked in the mild slanting morning sunlight and sipped margaritas. She relaxed after swimming and visualized what was in the store for her in the day ahead.

When she reached the dining hall, the breakfast was ready and it was properly arranged. It was steaming and odorous and its aroma was tempting. On the table, there were many varieties of delectable items, including south Indian, north Indian and continental. Everybody had arrived in the restaurant by this time. Vikas took an initiative to initiate conversation among the participants after introduction. This was an excellent opportunity to get introduced. All met and had animated conversation while enjoying tasty breakfast.

~~~~

As decided during breakfast, all had already reached central hall well before Vikas entered the hall. Sofia and Shams had already checked audio and video devices, which were properly functioning.

"I am happy all the participants have arrived and are present here, in this hall," said Vikas beaming a smile. "I welcome everybody. I hope, all of you are comfortable and having a wonderful time in your suites. If you still feel any difficulty, please let me know or you may directly communicate to Sofia and Shams. They are also here with us."

"Though we have made all the arrangements, yet we will be glad to extend any help, any time," articulated Shams convincingly with a mild smile. "We will always be in touch. There will always be some person available on intercom also."

"Please let us know, if we can be of any help," interjected Sofia. "Even if we are at our houses, we will be available on phone."

"Our main purpose to congregate here this moment is to have a brief introduction and interaction with each other. We are going to meet formally tomorrow," said Vikas.

"Where and at what time should we assemble?" enquired John with intrinsic curiosity.

"In this hall only. There is no hurry. Take your own time to get ready, by 8-30. We will spend our day here in this central hall," explained Vikas. "We will do relaxing meditation and discuss: 'Intention and purpose' and 'Tough minded Dynamic Optimism'. We will float through our day with an effortless ease, with amusing baby steps. We will have our lunch on the 'Tree Top Restaurant' in the forest. Then we will come back here and will work till 6 in the evening."

"Do not you think the schedule is hectic and too tiring?" queried Reena taking deep sigh.

"Not at all," shot back Vikas with smile and with a measure of certainty. "All of you are going to have an exotic and wonderful experience at 'Tree Top'. It will not be a normal lunch, but we will practice 'Food Meditation' there. You will relish memory of every moment spent there. This workshop is structured in such a manner, you are going to enjoy every moment here on this resort. All the activities here are going to be fun."

"Wow!" Reena exclaimed with joy.

"In the evening, there is an arrangement for body massage for ladies and gentlemen separately," Vikas expatiated with a smile after a brief pause.

"Wow… how wonderful!" squeaked Mitali delightedly. "We all will feel relaxed, stress-free, happy and free from fatigue."

"How wondrous!" Reena exclaimed joyfully. "That will be an awesome experience and a great relaxing break."

"Yes, Reena," said Vikas with jubilantly. "Do you still feel that the day is going to be boring and hectic?"

"No," mumbled Reena with a meek smile. "We will feel immense joy and thrill."

"Welcome everybody in the first day of workshop. Today is going to be a wonderful day. I want your full participation to make this workshop successful, as it is an interactive workshop. Please involve me also, if you have to discuss something. Keep your mobiles in silence mode. I want minimum distraction and focused participation," articulated Vikas. "Interact more and practice more. Noble ideas are useful, only if you implant them in others mind and put them into practice. We are going to interact often and live here every moment with bliss and joy."

"I think, before we start the workshop, we should know more about each other. But I want slightly different type of introduction here," explained Vikas. "Choose a partner and interact with each other, and then you introduce your partner to the participants in front of everybody in this workshop."

"It is a magnificent and unique idea," articulated Sofia with a smile, "to introduce this way."

"You are all attending this workshop with some purpose in your mind, are not you?" asked Vikas.

"Yes, of course," said Vinod.

"I will like to know that purpose," asked Vikas. "Will you like to tell me, what do you want out of this workshop?"

"I want a break from adventurous life and relax so that I am full of vigor and energy to be more adventurous," squeaked Vinod with a smile. "I want a brief respite and a healthy change from daily routine."

"You will get what you passionately desire. Find out your passion, focus your attention on it, till your subconscious takes over. Release your passionate desires to the universe. The universe will deliver the same to you in its own time. Have faith in God. You will go back, infused with more vigor and vitality to perform better in life."

"I am a doctor and my passion is to help as many people as possible. If I combine medicine, treatment with unconditional love and motivation, I will be able to serve in a better manner," articulated Dr. Meena with a smile. "I also want motivation to continue with perseverance in face of difficulties and uncertainties."

"I have noticed that you have an inordinate passion and a magnificent desire to serve others. I am sure this workshop is for you, Dr. Meena," uttered Vikas. "You are all from different fields of life and have different types of experiences. You all will be enriched by interacting frequently and sharing you experiences with each other. Everybody has something to contribute. This workshop will give boost to your accomplishments in all the areas of your life, at the same time, it will provide you inner joy, and enhance your personal growth and jest for life," reiterated Vikas reassuringly. "As you have expressed, we all face daily tensions related to our work, traveling and family. We all require persistent motivation to continue, to pursue our desires and to live a fabulous life."

"We all have wonderful ideas, but we can reap real benefits, only if we interact and share more," added Vikas, "We are all going to be enriched through smooth conversations to a great extent. You will exchange so many ideas, which are interesting, elevating, inspiring and enriching. You will learn so many valuable things from each other. Sometimes, however you will, doubtless, also hear that is unexciting. The richest ores contain dross. So, my dear friends, interact and discuss freely, whenever you feel to do so and make the best of this wonderful workshop. But, I reiterate, please involve me also in your discussions."

"Mitali, please introduce your partner," said Vikas after a pause.

"Reena is an old friend of mine. She is a beautiful and a glamorous model and an adroit actress," Mitali introduced joyfully, while everybody listened with an intrinsic curiosity. "She is participating in this workshop for the first time. She never had an experience of such a workshop earlier. She is an energetic lady with a positive mental attitude. Sometimes she feels that something is lacking in her and this lack disrupts her serenity and poise. She is attending this workshop to live a stress-free life and achieve inner quietude."

"Your job is full of glamor. You might be meeting so many interesting people and having wonderful experiences, right? You require faith, hope and stamina to move ahead in life," said Vikas reassuringly with a measure of certainty. "You have correctly decided, Reena, to attend this workshop. It is certainly going to be enriching and it will be of enormous help to you in your personal and professional life. If you sincerely follow the ideas, we are going to discuss here, your life will be metamorphosed for better. You will discover and manifest your best."

Sofia gesticulated to speak.

"Yes Sofia, please go ahead." Vikas encouraged her. "Please introduce Mr. John."

"Mr. John is a successful business man. He is a sports man and an international Tennis player. He is a voracious reader and he studies a lot, especially personality literature, for his self-growth. He feels that he will get here an opportunity to put principles and ideas into practice and change his attitude for better and meaningful life," prattled Sofia. "He, sometimes, feels miserable. He feels that he is not happy. He has lot of money, but satisfaction, contentment and peace of mind is missing in his life."

"Welcome Mr. John," Vikas chimed in, looking at him with a smile. "I understand your problem. This is an interactive workshop. You will get opportunity to put your ideas into practice. I advise you to take initiative to interact more. From one person you will learn one thing; from another something else. Put these shreds together, and in time you will form quite a number of pages in the great book of your life."

"Thanks, Mr. Vikas," said John.

"You should discuss all the problems of general nature here. I reiterate, discuss as much as possible and put ideas into practice. If you require some discussion of personal nature, we may have one-to-one interaction during some evenings," Vikas elaborated. "We will arrange evening rendezvous for discussion of problems of personal nature soon."

"Thanks, Mr. Vikas," said John. "I have to discuss some personal problems with you."

"Mr. John, I will help you solve your personal problem after thorough analysis and discussing in detail."

"Thank you very much, Vikas."

"Dr. Meena, please introduce your partner," said Vikas.

"Mr. Vinod is a charming and adventurous personality. He is a customs officer and sailing is his hobby. He has got his own luxury boat. You all will be flabbergasted to know that he has sailed to this resort by his own boat. He is a very active and practical person, but he wants to be spiritually enriched as well," articulated Dr. Meena.

"Positive interactions enrich all," articulated Vikas reassuringly. "We will all be richer spiritually too. To live a meaningful life, we should be adventurous and active, at the same time we should be free from stress. Time to time, we should relax with peaceful mind to regain energy to gallop ahead with more vigor."

"Thank you very much," said Vinod.

"Before we proceed further, let us visualize a marvelous day ahead. Let us first sit relaxed and do deep breathing… Sit comfortably, please… Inhale slowly and exhale completely with effortless ease… Relax all parts of your body… one by one… Breathe naturally with an effortless ease… Do not try to alter your breathing… just observe inflow and outflow… Decide now, what you want to get out of this day," explained Vikas and demonstrated, sitting relaxed. "Now set your intention of the day."

"I am sorry to interrupt, Vikas," interposed Sofia. "What do you mean by setting intention?"

"Very good question, Sofia," remarked Vikas encouragingly. "Intentions are insightful statements about the way you want to live your life. They elucidate how you want to be and live in this world. They delineate core principles on which you base your decisions and actions when you are confronted with challenges of life. Is it clear Sofia?"

"Yes, thank you Vikas."

"Visualize an excellent day ahead… Do it now and take your own time… There is no hurry… Set intention of the day… Visualize with hassle-free and happy mind how your day will be, and what you are going to do during this day… Visualize, exactly with minute detail, how wonderful your day will be," said Vikas. "Be a tough-minded optimist."

Everybody listened with concentration and followed the instructions religiously.

"Before we proceed further, please write down 5 blessings you have, 5 plus points in your personality, 5 persons you love most and 5 persons you hate most and 5 passionate desires you want to fulfill in your life. There is no need to reveal this data to others, so keep it with you. It will be handy and helpful during our further discussions."

"Now come to the carpet and sit down comfortably. Be totally present and be totally focused in the moment. Do not think about past and future. Breathe easily and naturally, till you feel totally relaxed. Breathe slowly, steadily, naturally and with an effortless ease and try to completely relax your mind and body. Continue, till you feel totally relaxed and your senses start responding efficiently," explained Vikas. "You will be more creative when relaxed."

"You have here, in front of you, colored pencils, stickers, white sheets and erasers. Express yourself and your creativity on the sheet. Make any shape you like. You may draw a scenery, flower or anything you like," said Vikas. "You are all born artists. Manifest your endowments here and now."

Everybody took his seat and started, as they were told to do.

"Focus your attention here, in the activity you are doing. We do not know what is going to happen next moment," explained Vikas. "We are bound to worry to some extent about unpredictable future. Something favorable may happen and also something unfavorable may happen. Live fully in the present moment."

"Yes, we feel miserable visualizing bad possibilities. It is, therefore, always advisable to live in the present moment, without thinking much about past and future," asserted Reena.

"The present moment is the only moment when you can effectively live," interjected Dr. Meena.

"We cannot totally avoid thinking about past and future," asserted John. "Our identity is defined by what we did in the past and our life is going to be what we plan about future."

"Thank you Reena and Dr. Meena. You are correct. Past is good for learning from our mistakes and future is good for planning, as you suggested, but you can live only in the present moment," said Vikas encouragingly. "Make, therefore, your dwelling place in this moment."

"Okay," said John.

"But make sure, when you plan or think about future, you must do so with faith and hope," elaborated Vikas. "You should think with a positive mental attitude and be a tough-minded dynamic optimist."

"I understand optimism, but what is tough-minded dynamic optimism?" enquired Reena with curiosity. "I know that optimism is thinking about favorable outcomes."

"Can you give an example," Vikas chimed in, with a smile.

"Suppose I am on a date and waiting at a lonely beach. Somehow my boyfriend gets late. I, deliberately, think that he will certainly come," mumbled Reena with a charming smile, "and we will have wonderful time together. Now please, tell me what a tough-minded optimism is."

"Who is that lucky boyfriend, Reena?" cooed Mitali. "Can you delineate, how you were going to have a wonderful time together?"

"*Shut up Mitali. How you can be so naughty?*" Reena thought, blushing profusely, but said nothing.

Everyone laughed joyfully.

"Attention here and now, please," Vikas interjected trying in to change the topic. "When you are optimist, you do not allow the optimism to fade even in face of adverse circumstances."

"You resolutely use your awareness and will-power to remain optimist. That is a tough-minded optimism," delineated Vikas lucidly. "If, in spite of your best efforts, the desired outcome is not coming forth and you take an effective, dynamic, result oriented and positive action to make that thing happen; that is 'tough-minded dynamic optimism.' By your dynamic action you make the things happen."

"You have clearly explained, Vikas," articulated Sofia. "It is now amply clear. Thank you very much."

Chapter-3

"We discussed enough and now let us enjoy the lunch break. As I told you earlier, there is a marvelous tree top restaurant in deep forest, a few minutes' walk from here. It is a peaceful place in a natural setting, surrounded by huge green trees and bushes with fragrant flowers galore. It is a serene place suitable for meditation. Let us go there for lunch," delineated Vikas. "That location is superb and you all will love it. It is so peaceful; you will hear only chirping of birds and rustle of leaves from surrounding trees."

It was a beautiful experience to walk in the green forest. Everybody enjoyed walking in the natural environment. The dense forest, amid which they traversed, was desolate and wild in the extreme. There was absolutely no sign of a human being, or their habitation of any sort. There was no sound except for the steady sound of the stream of a nearby river mingled with the sound of howling of wind in trees and chirping of birds.

The scenery, with its accompaniments, was abundantly verdant and soothing. The narrow serpentine river flowing through the dense and interminable forest looked marvelous and fascinating. Huge trees provided comforting shade. The tree top restaurant was erected on three huge trees on a small hill. It did not take much time to ascend to reach the place.

There was a wooden ladder leading to beautiful tree top. Seating arrangement was wonderful. There was a round comfortable sofa on which 10 persons could easily sit. There was a big round central table in the middle. Red carpet on stairs and floor in verdant location looked magnificent. The place was full of vegetation and fragrant flowers. Cold breeze was blowing. Sound of rustle of leaves combined with chirping of birds, creating soothing music. The river looked beautiful from the top.

"I never imagined that this place would be so beautiful," squeaked Reena with jubilation. "I am happy I decided to attend this workshop."

"I am happy you like this place," muttered Vikas. "I liked this place at the first sight when I visited this place earlier."

"You told that you are here for food meditation. How can we meditate while eating," asked Mitali inquisitively, while washing her hands in wash basin. "Meditation is not simple practice, as it requires lot of concentration and awareness."

"Meditation is not difficult. You can meditate, even if you are doing simplest mundane work," Vikas shot back. "Swami Sivananda appropriately said, *Put your heart, mind, and soul into even your smallest acts. This is the secret of successes.*"

"What are you doing?" asked Vikas after a brief pause.

"Washing hands, of course," replied Mitali.

"You are, probably, not aware of activity you are doing now. Are you?" asked Vikas. "You are doing it in a conditioned manner, without awareness and without paying much attention."

"You are correct, Vikas," said Mitali. "I am doing it, as I generally do, just as a routine work, without awareness."

"Relax, pause and deep breathe. Slow down and focus your attention on washing hand. Feel the smell, weight and smoothness of soap. Also feel temperature and softness of water. You may briefly close your eyes, if you like to intensify your awareness."

"Okay," murmured Mitali with a smile, closing her eyes. She followed his instructions.

"Can you feel it now?" asked Vikas. "Continue."

"Yes," said Mitali.

"Now, please open your eyes and come slowly here, paying attention on every step you take and sit down here." expatiated Vikas with a smile. "During this time did you listen chirping of bird?"

"No, I was concentrating on washing of hand, as you suggested."

"That time you were oblivious of what is happening around."

"Yes, I realize it," said Mitali.

"Now sit relaxed, take a steady and deep breath and close your eyes again. Focus your attention on the sound of chirping of birds and rustle of leaves in the trees," said Vikas.

"Okay," said Mitali. Everybody listened with interest.

"Can you recognize 5 different sounds?" Vikas asked. "Take your own time. There is no hurry… How do you feel?"

"I never realized earlier that there is meditation in simple activities," Mitali muttered. "I feels terrific and wonderful."

"Every simple activity can be a meditation with focus and awareness," reiterated Vikas. "If you do your work with full concentration and in a contemplative way, you do not have to do meditation separately. Einstein was, generally, so much engrossed in his work, he used to forget to take his food."

"Come here everybody. Sit with me comfortably on this sofa, relaxed," advised Vikas after a pause. All complied with his instructions. "I am going to do Eating Meditation or Food Meditation."

"What is that? Can you describe it?" asked Mitali interestedly with curiosity. "I have never heard about it earlier."

"Eating Meditation is one of the simplest and most insightful of meditative practices, you can perform," explained Vikas. "It is practicable for you, irrespective of your faith and belief. You may be following any religion or you may have any or no religious background. It is so simple that you do not require any formal meditation experience."

Everybody looked at him eagerly, in a receptive mode.

"As usual, you may start with a deep, rhythmic and relaxed breathing. Continue for 10 minutes. It will profoundly relax your mind and you will be in the placid state," Vikas delineated. "Do it now. Mitali, you please guide the breathing and relaxing meditation."

"Please sit relaxed, feet squarely placed on the ground, eyes closed. Inhale for count of 5; 1, 2, 3, 4, 5 and let your lungs swell. Hold your breath for count of 3; 1, 2, 3. Now exhale completely, emptying your lungs for count of 5; 1, 2, 3, 4, 5," explained and demonstrated Mitali. Everybody followed her directions. "Now, you continue for 10 minutes or till you feel relaxed. Relax every part of your body from head to toe, focusing briefly on tense parts."

"Eating a meal together, as we are going to do now, in a focused and serene state, is an amazing meditative practice," said Vikas. "We are now relaxed and present here in the moment."

Vikas gestured toward Shams and then Shams in turn signaled to waiter, who was looking at him already. Waiter promptly brought huge trays, full of variety of food and put them in front of everybody, one by one. Aroma of hot delectable food mingled with cold breeze filtered through leaves of huge surrounding trees.

"Can you feel the odor?" asked Vikas. "Smell the aroma, inhaling deep, closing your eyes. Can you distinguish different types of fragrances?"

"Yes," replied Mitali sniffing and inhaling deep. "It is wonderful. I can distinguish 4 types."

"Okay, great. Now, everybody, open your eyes and look at the meal. Contemplate where this food came from. Imagine how it is prepared and who prepared it," said Vikas with gratitude.

The ambience was full of aroma of delicious food. Everybody appeared to be happy.

"It is not a simple food. In front of you, there is vitality of the sun and energy of the cloud. Rains, hard work, sunshine, earth, air and unconditional love have combined together to make this magnificent food," articulated Vikas, pronouncing every word distinctly with slow and relaxed pace. "Be grateful to God for this meal, as through this nourishment, the Almighty is sustaining our life. This food is a wonderful gift from the universe, the sun, the nature and the environment."

Everybody listened with a focused mind and followed his instructions religiously.

"Before you start taking the food, please bless the farmer, the laborer, the cook, the transporter and the waiter involved in bringing this food to you. Hard work of so many persons is involved in this food," added Vikas after a pause. Everybody listened attentively in a relaxed manner.

"Now repeat in your mind, "This food is worthy of being received, relished and accepted. I am in a receptive mode. I accept this food gratefully and gracefully, so that I may nurture myself, my family, my brotherhood and the humanity. With its help, we will keep our compassion alive by eating in such a way that we reduce the suffering of living beings, preserve our planet and reverse the process of global warming."

Everybody repeated.

"Aroma of food appears to be so delectable, it is irresistible to eat," Reena chuckled with smile. "When will the actual eating process be initiated?"

"You have not even felt it yet," Vikas chuckled with a joyful smile. "Now feel the food with your fingers. Do not eat it yet. Just look at it with awareness and concentrated attention. Perceive how it appears? Allow yourself the pleasure of being entranced by this."

He did not speak for almost a minute or so; then he continued, with his usual equanimity and relaxed demeanor, "Smell the food and notice its aroma again. Notice, how it affects the intensity of your hunger. Is it aggravating your hunger or diminishing it? Feel it in your fingers, paying attention to the sensual eminence of the food. Feel its temperature, quantity, texture, weight and character."

"I think, now your hunger is aroused. You may slowly and mindfully put the food in your mouth, but do not chew it yet. Simply feel the food on your tongue. Feel how it tastes before being chewed. Notice its temperature, smell and its texture on your tongue," explained Vikas. "Notice how your whole body changes and reacts to the food in your mouth. See how the salivation begins."

"This meal is going to affect your body and mind. Observe what happens to your whole body when you put the food in. Pay close attention to the entire process. Now observe how the stomach becomes active. You may open or close your eyes, as you like," elaborated Vikas in detail. "Slowly and mindfully chew the food. Attempt to chew in an attentive and active manner. As much as possible, keep your attention on the food and the act of chewing it. Be present in the moment and let go of all other thoughts."

"Closing your eyes may be helpful, time to time. Be aware when you bite into the food and chew and know that you are chewing," expatiated and reiterated Vikas in detail with his usual composure. "Eat slowly, experience gastronomic and olfactory delight, and do not gulp down your food. We should take our time, as we eat, chewing each mouthful at least 30 times, until the food mingles with the saliva and becomes liquefied. This helps the digestive process. Swallow, after the food has been thoroughly chewed, probably twenty to thirty times."

"Observe, if the flavor of food changes, as you continue and when you swallow. Notice and feel the food going down your esophagus," Vikas uttered softly as he also ate the food. "Just relax and enjoy the physical sensations of eating every morsel of your food, being in the present moment."

"I think, we all have finished our food," mumbled John softly. "It is a fantastic experience. I, really, enjoyed the meal. I noticed so many things, I never noticed before in my life. I was ecstatic."

"Because we generally do things in automatic, preset and conditioned manner," Vikas expatiated. "Now, take a few moments to notice that you have finished, your plates are empty and your craving is fulfilled. Express your gratitude to God for delectable, aromatic and nourishing food."

"I entreat you to make eating meditation a regular part of your day, for 21 days, till it becomes your habit. It takes around 21 days form a new habit," explained Vikas. "Believe it or not, people practicing food meditation report deep contentment, joy and insight into their personalities and immense gratitude to God!"

"How do you feel, Dr. Meena?"

"It is a wonderful practice. It is also a very effective and simple meditation technique. It is going to help me a lot in my daily life and in my professional career. These practices are more important than medicines," said Dr. Meena. "This practice will also help reduce the pace of eating, which will help better digestion of food and reduce the excess weight."

"I had a wonderful experience, taking food that way. I will never forget this beautiful experience," mumbled Vinod. "I am going to practice it regularly."

~~~~

"Let us now go down stairs and stroll around in the forest with slow pace. Then we will go back again to central hall to discuss about mission, vision and purpose."

All had good time strolling around in the green forest. All of them walked slowly up to the Central Hall for the afternoon rendezvous.

"I hope everybody is back."

"Yes," Reena chirped smiling, entering in the hall. "I am the last one."

"Defining and expounding your life purpose and core life intentions can help you move with enhanced focus and clarity in every day of your life," said Vikas. "Especially in these challenging times, setting the clear intentions and developing and redefining our life purpose can make it much easier to sail through stormy waters. There are many ways to both find and develop your life purpose and intentions."

"But how can we find or define our purpose?" asked Sofia inquisitively.

"Sofia, I am coming to that. Asking questions is the most effective way to explore your mind and find your vision. Without vision you will be moving like a rudderless boat. If you do not know your destination, no road is the right road. You should know the general direction in which you have to move," explained Vikas. "Ask yourself, where you want to be in a week, a month, a year, 5 years and 10 years? How you want to be remembered? What is most important to you? What are your passionate desires, which you want to accomplish before you breathe your last breath? What are your important goals, visions and missions in life?"

"Give yourself time to explore these important questions and notice what touches and inspires you most deeply. Write down any answers or thoughts that come to you as you ponder these questions."

"Honestly answer these questions to yourself and note down the intrinsic message," explained Vikas. "Explore your heart to find the answer. Carl Jung had said: *'Your vision will become clear only when you can look into your own heart. Who looks outside, dreams; who looks inside, awakes.'* Then, after perspicacious analysis, you can take an effective action"

Vikas turned towards the board and drew 2 inverted 'U' shapes on the board and asked participants, "Can anybody guess what they are?"

Nobody could guess anything. All looked at each other.

"These are two tombstone, one erected by you for yourself and the other too for you, but erected by others. Draw these two tombstones on your notebook now and write your epitaph on both the tombstones, one you would write for yourself and the other you think the others will write for you. Everybody, do it now," explained Vikas.

"What do you learn from this exercise, Dr. Meena?" asked Vikas.

"This exercise clearly illuminates how you will like to be remembered after death," explained Dr. Meena. "It helps us find out purpose of our life."

"Yes, you are correct," said Vikas.

"It helped me to think in a different way to find the purpose of life and the lasting values I should develop," John interjected. "This exercise also inspired me to ponder, how I want to be remembered after my death."

"Sometimes we decide our aims and goals, but we soon forget them," asserted Shams. "How can we constantly keep these ideas in mind?"

"Once you find and develop your life purpose, vision, missions and intentions, write them on a piece of paper, on computer or on a board. Then consider finding a suitable place where you can refer them, time to time," said Vikas. "Review them each day, awakening in the morning, to help you constantly keep in your mind during the day. You should also review them just before going to sleep. If you review them time to time, your subconscious will take over and you will move more effectively and powerfully through the day."

"Okay," said Sofia. "What other practices are helpful?"

"Take help of mind mapping and vision board," said Vikas. "Once your life purpose and intentions become clearer, your life is likely to move more smoothly in the desired direction."

"Thank you very much, Vikas," said Sofia.

"When your purpose is clear in your mind, you can easily achieve it. Your life will become more abundant as you move with enhanced determination, focus, and intention," explained Vikas. "By frequently reminding yourself of your purpose and intentions, you become more focused and effective in building a brighter future for yourself and for those all around you."

"What is mind-mapping?" asked Vinod curiously, "and what is vision board? How can I prepare a vision board?"

"Mind-mapping is a planning technique. Here we use drawings, lines, maps and images to effectively plan and display our vision and missions. We can use mind-mappings or visualization techniques to reflect and plan your week and day," elucidated Vikas. "It is better than note taking."

"How mind mapping is better than conventional note taking?" asked Shams.

"Firstly, they are more compact than conventional notes. Secondly, they are also helpful to make associations easily, and generate new ideas," expatiated Vikas. "If you find out more information to add, you can easily incorporate it with the original mind-map without any problem. Mind-mapping also helps us breaking large projects into manageable chunks. We can plan more effectively and efficiently without being overwhelmed," explained Vikas after a brief pause, with his usual candor.

"A comprehensive mind-map shows the 'shape' of the subject, the relative importance of individual points, and the way in which facts relate to one another. Remembering the shape and structure of a mind-map can give you the cues you need to remember the information within it."

"What is a vision board?" asked John. "How can we make it?"

"It is an assortment of imageries, sketches, clippings from newspapers and avowals of your dreams and all of the things that make you joyful. Vision board can also be called a dream board, or treasure map," explained Vikas. "For making it, we use attractive images, pictures and drawings and to make our cherished desires clear. To be specific, we may paste in it, photos of our desired car and our dream house. The vision board constantly reminds us about our passions and motivates us to action."

"What is secret behind its effectiveness?" asked Meena.

"Vision boards are helpful because 'like thoughts attract like thoughts'. They make us feel positive and motivated. By referring time to time and focusing on the items on the board, you can manifest them easily. Visual images generate feelings, which are more effective than thoughts."

"Very interesting indeed. I am curious to know more. What other points should I keep in mind while making vision board?" asked Dr. Meena. "How should I actually prepare it?"

"To begin with, decide the main theme of your board. You may have specific or general passions to achieve. It may be something that makes you happy and meaningful. Then arrange images from magazines and Internet that are in conformity with your theme," delineated Vikas. "You may stick images and affirmations to the board. With practice, you will be able to create interesting stories. Make sure to place your board in a place you will easily see. View your board at least once a day and focus on the objects, sayings and theme of your board."

~~~~

Dr. Meena was tired when she reached her suite. She took shower and she was lying in the bath tub when she got a call on the intercom.

"Hi Dr. Meena. How are you? I hope I have not disturbed you. Are you free now?" asked Vinod.

"Not exactly, but I will be fresh in half an hour," replied Dr. Meena, suppressing her happiness. She was thinking about him when she got the call. "Why are you asking?"

"I want to take coffee with you, if you do not mind."

"Where?"

"In the lawn of the restaurant."

"Okay," mumbled Dr. Meena after a pause with hesitation. She gave her usual tacit reply.

"I will wait for you," said Vinod in a joyful mood.

"Okay."

Vinod was happy to meet Dr. Meena. In fact he wanted to sit with her and talk to her. He liked her soft nature. She was rarely participating in general conversation. He found her usually silent and he liked her taciturnity. He noticed some changes in her behavior, since he started taking interest in her and he incited her to interact more.

Vinod reached a bit earlier. He found a quiet table that overlooked the lush lawns. He was glad to see her coming.

"Hi, Dr. Meena," Vinod galloped ahead to receive her. "Thanks for coming. I was eagerly waiting for you."

"It is my pleasure. I was also eager to meet you and talk to you," said Dr. Meena with smile. She looked beautiful in light blue sari. Her strands were hanging and brushing her face. "I hesitate to communicate more often because of my tacit nature. I want to overcome this personality defect."

"This is not a defect. It is a type of personality. I like such personality. Be yourself and do not seek approval of others."

"Thank you very much, Vinod," said Meena, for liking me the way I am. "Probably, this is why I feel comfortable with you. I believe in TCEFB, TNU, and EBBOM."

"Strange acronyms," Vinod murmured with a smile, "can you explicate?"

"Talk 'Concisely, Effectively, Forcefully and Boldly'… Speak only what is 'True, Necessary, and Useful'… 'Engage Brain Before Opening Mouth'.

"Very interesting. I have observed that you talk less but your comments are wise and appropriate," muttered Vinod appreciatingly. "Tell me what you will like to have."

"I will like to have light snacks with coffee," whispered Dr. Meena with a butter-soft voice, gaining composure. She was feeling more comfortable now.

"I discontinued giving advice years ago, but I will venture to give you a suggestion in my own interest. I entreaty you not to be so cold and so exceedingly laconic today or whenever you are with me alone," cooed Vinod after a brief pause. His voice appeared amicable and persuasive. "I want to talk to you to my heart's content."

"You are the first person to like me the way I am. You made me feel important and brimming with self-esteem. I do not know why but I also feel like talking to you often," she asserted smiling. "What attracts you in a tacit person?"

"Taciturnity is the only tangible thing we can hold in this world of ephemeral dreams. Time is a like shadow that will vanish with the twilight of humanity; but silence is, on the other hand a part of the eternal. Silence is a quality which everybody does not have," said Vinod convincingly. "One who talks relentlessly has a thousand ways always at his hand in which to make a fool of himself. A silent person, on the other hand, has not even single. Generally you will find people who think that he is silent because of his wisdom. All things that are true, important and lasting have been taught to us by silence."

"Wonderful philosophy. You are charismatic and a wonderful person." mumbled Meena with a charming smile, sneaking a loving look at him. "I feel happy and comfortable in your presence."

"It is my pleasure."

"You made me happy and enhanced my self-esteem," chuckled Meena with twinkling eyes. She realized that she was no more laconic today and the words were tumbling down from her tongue easily uninterrupted.

"I or you can elicit only what is within," muttered Vinod with a lovely smile. "If you are happy, it is nothing to do with my presence. It is your own reaction to my presence and my suggestion. Reaction is always in your hand. It is your life and you are responsible for your thoughts, feelings, actions and reactions."

"Wonderful thoughts," clucked Meena with joy. Her personal consciousness, by now, was almost lost in the intense curiosity which the circumstances had aroused in her. "I am impressed. I never expected such an ideology from a Customs Officer."

"It has nothing to do with the profession. All depends on the company one keeps, the sources of inspiration and exposure. Such workshops, as we are attending now a days, are very helpful in formation of positive ideology."

"Wow! You have attended such workshops earlier also?" exclaimed Dr. Meena, her eyes sparkled with curiosity. "After attending this workshop, I realize that I should also have attended a few more of them."

"Yes, I attended different types of workshops," said Vinod. "Such workshops have tremendous impact on the attitude and personality."

"I agree, as I notice it in your personality."

"I am glad to meet you here today," cooed Vinod zestfully. "In fact, I had been eager to meet you, since I saw you for the first time."

"Really? Do not tell me! Are you kidding?" retorted Dr. Meena with a charming smile. "What is so special in me?"

"That is what I am eager to find out," said Vinod, with a jubilant smile, looking into her eyes deeply, "if you let me explore."

"Please let me know, if you notice something," chuckled Dr. Meena. "I do not think I have anything special in me. I like your sense of humor and your adventurous spirit. May be this is the reason, I was also eager to meet you."

"Really? I am happy to know that," squeaked Vinod extending his hand across the table to shake with her. Both shook hands. "From today onward, we are going to be good friends."

"Yes Vinod," chuckled Dr. Meena with a gorgeous smile. "I relished your company. Thanks for coffee and the doughnut. Please keep in touch."

Chapter-4

Vikas had always been an early riser, so he rose with the sun. He opened the windows to allow the fresh breeze enter. The sun rose so placidly and smiled so compassionately that his fatigue disappeared, in spite of all that had happened on the previous day. The storm, which had brought some discomfort the night before, had subsided considerably. The rains settled the ground and made it comparatively firm. After getting fresh, he took a few rounds in the wet verdant lawn.

He got ready to start the day, as he envisioned. Everybody had arrived to his place. All were in a joyful mood to greet the day. They were ready for sojourn, according to his instructions.

"Good morning friends. Today we are going to Serenity Lake by cars. We will be there whole day and have our lunch there only," said Vikas. "This lake is a marvelous natural location. There is a small elevated land in center of lake. We will have our workshop there in a temporarily erected tent."

"Wow we are going to have one more fantabulous day," squeaked Mitali with ebullient delight. "Vikas, I will never forget this exquisite visit and workshop on this island resort."

"Thanks Mitali," said Vikas. "I am sure, all of you will have a fabulous time there."

All of them reached the place in 50 minute. The view was magnificent. It was the clearest and freshest morning that they could ever wish for and the grass was still wet. It had been raining incessantly since the yesterday afternoon.

Then there was a thunder storm in the night. It had continued raining till morning.

As they reached a few miles before the destination, they began to catch glimpses of the lake flanked by small hills through the trees. Its blue stretch of water was shining in the morning sun. It looked like a blue diamond set in the dull brown gold of woods and fields.

The violent thunder-storm, which thundered and flared in early morning, had subsided and rolled away by that time. The wind had, by now, died away and the forest was still. The brisk and fresh breeze had blown the sky clear. Now, only a few small patches of clouds were floating in the sky. They were creating gorgeous golden images in the clear blue sky.

A few small patches of the morning mist, however, hung about the trees and bushes. The sun was gradually rising up in the sky illuminating grass land. It had risen by now and the moisture had nearly disappeared, except in the grass and bushes. Some rain drops still sparkled on the grass. It was a wonderful day and there was promise of terrific day ahead.

The lake looked beautiful. The sun had risen in full magnificence from behind the hills. An all-encompassing mirror of water had opened upon their view. All walked on a path around the beautiful large lake. They looked at each other in speechless, dazed amazement. It was delightful to see rippling water sparkling in the brilliant sunlight. The shadows of the huge trees were vividly reflected on the mirror-like clear surface near the bank of lake. The lake was full of pink lotuses flanked by green leaves. Rain left the green leaves and grass lands sweetly smelling and glistening, which pleased everybody's eyes. Presence of white ducks made the ambience even more fantabulous.

"See how wonderful these ducks are. They are flapping their wings, as if they are joyously welcoming you Shams. I never imagined earlier that frogs can croak so melodiously. There is a magical music in their sweet guttural sound," squeaked Sofia joyously smiling charmingly at Shams. "These lotuses… wow!"

He was astounded at her romantic insinuations.

"Yes Sofia. This is one of the three small lakes that adorn these landscapes. It is about half a mile long, half as wide. It is constantly fed by nine springs. This is always filled with sparkling fresh water," ejaculated Shams, simply looking at her with adoring eyes, with constant gaze. "You seem to be very romantic today."

"Thank you Shams," cooed Sofia blushing profusely. "I always feel wonderful in your presence, in such a natural ambience."

"You look even more charming, when you blush, Sofia," said Shams looking deep in to her eyes, lovingly. A joyful expression smiled in her eyes and dimpled over the whole visage. She regained her composure and laughed with delight.

"You presence in my life means a lot to me. It gives me real contentment, my dear Sofia, when I see you joyful. Keep laughing and enjoying your life. Laughter clings to good health as naturally as a needle clings to a magnet. It is an outward expression of inner bliss."

There was a narrow walking path around the lake strewn with green bushes and fragrant flowers. Colorful butterflies were tremendously enhancing the beauty of flamboyant flowers. There were birds galore tweeting in the trees and the bushes nearby. Blended song of the birds was very soothing and pleasing. Swarms of bees were humming over the colorful flowers. Everybody was happy to see a flock of swans passing over at a height on their long journey.

"See, how wonderful is this location, Dr. Meena," squeaked Vinod from behind. "Very romantic indeed. Is not it?"

"Yes, it is stunning. I love this place. I am very much fond of lakes. They are even more soothing than rivers or the sea. Rivers are always moving unceasingly. The sea may be sometimes calm and composed, but is generally full of enormous dynamism. Lakes, on the other hand, are placid and unruffled, most of the time," Cooed Meena with her brighter than ever smile. "This fresh water lake is superb."

"I agree with you Dr. Meena. From higher places they give the impression of charming blue crystals. Lakes are like diamonds in the necklace and sparkling eyes in a beautiful face," chuckled Vinod looking deep into her charming eyes, with his lips curved into a smile. "It is really a romantic place fit for honeymoon."

"It is so romantic that I will like to visit this place again someday," said Meena.

"For honeymoon?" asked Vinod with a naughty smile.

"You appear to be all the time in a honeymoon mood," Meena jested. She had at last yielded to laughter after a long-controlled excitement. Laughter had now entirely overcome her and she was in a joyful mood.

"Is it your private joke or we can also participate?" squeaked Mitali interrupting from behind, guffawing zestfully. "Sorry to eavesdrop, but who is going to celebrate honeymoon here?"

"Dr. Meena has such plans," cooed Vinod with a smile, looking at Mitali, pointing his finger toward Meena. "She feels that this location fit for her honeymoon."

"Not me… Mr. Vinod is not only planning, but vicariously enjoying his honeymoon here," retorted Dr. Meena blushing with a feeble smile. This time she took a little longer to regain her usual composure and looked menacingly into the eyes Vinod, wondering whether he really uttered those words. "Mitali, Mr. Vinod is all the time in honeymoon mood."

"There is absolutely no denying the fact that you both love this place, so you both should visit this place on honey moon," chuckled Mitali with a naughty smile. "It is up to you whether you visit separately with some other partners or you both visit together as partners of each other. Law of attraction works better, when there is synchro-destiny."

"What is synchro-destiny?" asked Meena. Her eyes lit up with an expression of acute curiosity.

"I will tell you," interjected Vikas, laughing loudly, galloping swiftly from behind. Everybody laughed joyfully. "When passionate desires of two or more persons combine in perfect harmony, they attract wonderful results. Law of Attraction works better, when frequencies match and fortunes are in synchronicity. We get our cherished desires fulfilled faster and get spectacular results."

"Okay," said Meena. "Now it is amply clear. Thank you Vikas."

"Mitali, do not you think that this place is beautiful and worth another visit?" chuckled Vinod with smile. "We rarely get an opportunity to visit such a wonderful place."

"I agree, Vinod," said Mitali with a smile. "Lakes are more serene and placid than rivers or the sea. I love such beautiful lakes. This lake is wonderful."

"These are like shining eyes on a beautiful face," added Vinod.

"Indeed, Vinod," Mitali mumbled. "As we gaze down from some cliff, it looks like a pearl necklace."

"Let us board the boat to Venue," said Vikas.

It was a wonderful experience to sail together in a beautiful lake. Everybody was fresh, relaxed and in a jubilant mood. The spot was beautiful and well maintained. All moved around and had coffee and snacks before entering the tent. All sat on comfortable chairs.

"Today we are going to discuss very important topic," said Vikas with an enthusiastic smile. "We all have resentments and grudges against somebody. These antipathies bother us for a considerably long time and they sap our energy, which we can, otherwise, utilize for some positive accomplishments."

"Yes, but it is natural." said Shams.

"Not natural," retorted Vikas. "It is a conditioned response and learned behavior."

"How?" asked Shams with curiosity.

"I will come to that," Vikas said. "Forgiveness, on the other hand, is a medicine, which re-establishes peace of mind. Forgiving, therefore, leads to harmony and bliss, as keeping grudge may consume your mental peace and disrupt natural thought process."

"Yes, we all have such feelings which constantly bother us. They are so deep rooted, we are not able to do anything to eliminate such feelings of resentment," asserted Sofia.

"We can easily eliminate such feelings. We can re-think and overcome such feelings and fill our minds with unconditional love," explained Vikas reassuringly. "We can forgive and forget."

"Is it really possible?" asked Mitali, enquiringly with suspicion. "I tried to release my mind by forgiving, but I failed. How can I forget when I cannot forgive?"

"You will do it here only and I will tell you how to do that. First you have to sincerely forgive, only then you can forget," affirmed Vikas convincingly with smile with a measure of certainty. "Still, if somebody is not successful, we will have later one-to-one session."

"Do not you think, people will treat it as weakness and they will become audacious to walk over us?" asked Reena.

"No, on the other hand, forgiveness is a sign of strength. Only a strong person can say 'sorry' and an even stronger person can forgive. Mahatma Gandhi expressed: '*The weak can never forgive. Forgiveness is the attribute of the strong.*' We all should, therefore, develop and maintain an attitude of forgiveness and we should forgive all at the earliest," advised Vikas. "Holding unexpressed resentment or grudges lowers our own positive vibrations and our ability to be cheerful and contented."

"Imagine you are holding a burning coal in your hand to throw it on someone else," Vikas elucidated further. "Who will be hurt?"

"Of course, I will be hurt," replied Mitali. "I will suffer most."

"You are correct. It is you who gets burnt. Forgiveness is, therefore, beneficial and it helps us in various ways," elucidated Vikas. "Forgiveness leads to healthier relationships, calming coziness and comforting effect."

"If the forgiveness is not accepted, what is its use?" asked Sofia.

"Still we get the emotional benefits," explicated Vikas. "We get mental peace and joy with tremendous cleansing effect. The people, to whom you forgive, may be constant source of help in future. It gives us mental peace, reduces the stress and helps us focus on more important things. It also helps us saving our time, money and energy, which is, otherwise, wasted on revenge. Robert Muller said: *'To forgive is the highest, most beautiful form of love. In return, you will receive untold peace and happiness.'* I entreat you, therefore, to forgive at the earliest opportunity."

"Sofia, an apology or forgiveness is always accepted, because it is useful for others too. You get an additional benefit, as it is beneficial for yourself too. When you forgive others, you do yourself a huge favor, because by doing this, you get rid of bitterness and negative feelings bottled up inside you," said Vikas. "Make your own peace your first priority and don't forget to put yourself on the top of your forgiveness list. It is painful to keep the hurt inside and suffocate yourself. When you forgive people, you do yourself a favor."

"Please tell me, how can I effectively forgive and forget?" asked John.

"Take an initiative. If there is someone you refuse to talk to, or harbor feelings of anger towards; phone him and write a letter to him. A letter of forgiveness is a significant positive step in the right direction," clarified Vikas. "It helps you in forgiving yourself by reducing repressed internal feelings of guilt. Explain your grounds, but don't make excuses for your behavior. Sincerely take responsibility for your actions. Make a sincere wish for the wellbeing of the person you hurt."

"I think controlling stress and anger is also helpful," elucidated Dr. Meena. "We should never allow stress to disturb our and others life. If you face a serious situation, like argument or a gratuitous and an unpleasant remark, analyze it with a positive mental attitude and sort out the problem there only. Steve Maraboli used to say: *'The truth is, unless you let go, unless you forgive yourself, unless you forgive the situation, unless you realize that that situation is over, you cannot move forward.'* You should immediately forgive yourself and the other person and also give the other person permission to forgive you."

"Awesome suggestion, Dr. Meena," said Vikas. "Analysis is very important. Ask yourself: Do you have a guilt feeling for something you did in the past? Are you angry with someone, who had physically abused you in the past? Today is a new day. Be contented and enjoy your life this moment. Ask for help from others. Accept that you made a mistake. It reduces stress and hostility, lowers blood pressure, mitigates symptoms of depression, anxiety and reduces chronic pain. Hopefully, it will make them and you less upset and more comfortable."

"Affirmation helps a lot. Words are powerful and should be, therefore, chosen and spoken with care. There are also words and phrases that can spoil your self-image, damage your reputation, and endanger your success. What we affirm to ourselves and say to others plays a dynamic role in helping us achieve victory and happiness. They are tools to help manifest our vision into reality."

Everybody was listening carefully with an amazing interest, lest they should miss a point.

"You are what you think all the day and what you constantly tell yourself all the day. Affirm, *'I sincerely forgive and wish all peace and bliss in life. I am calm and composed. I rest in safety and peace. I feel presence of supreme power within me. He is always with me to guide and protect me. God is always a good God. When he is with me, nothing can be against me. I am grateful to Him for all the blessings He has given me. I woke up alive and active today. He has given me one more wonderful day. I will rejoice and be joyful in it.'* Such affirmations create conducive environment for forgiveness."

elucidated Vikas. "Take responsibility for your mistakes. Forgiveness is more for your good, than for anyone else."

"With forgiveness you can achieve peace of mind. Forgive yourself and others at the first opportunity. It is win-win for all, as I have explained before. Forget what is over and forgive others and yourself. Ask for forgiveness from others," said Vikas. "Simple phrases like, 'Please forgive me; I am sorry, dear; thank you very much' have done more to hold family members in the home, to endear friends to each other and to comfort elders. They also placate lovers; and help marriages to be successful. Explain what you have done, why it is wrong and what you will do differently to prevent it from happening again."

"Should the letter of apology be posted," asked Vinod.

"It is not necessary to post it. It is up to you," explicated Vikas. "Post it, if you feel like doing so. It will be still better, if you discuss face to face. A face to face apology is always the most effective approach. Just try once to apologize to your family members for something you said or did in the past and see results for yourself."

"Do not be afraid to ask for forgiveness. If you don't ask, you will never feel the relief of being pardoned for your mistakes."

"Is there some more practical way of forgiving?" asked Reena.

"Yes I am coming to that," said Vikas. "First stand up and come out of the tent."

Everybody came out in open.

"Hang loose your hands," delineated Vikas. "Now vibrate and shake fast one hand… then the other hand… now both hands together… faster… raise one leg and vibrate vigorously and… the other legs… then both legs without raising… then whole body … I hope you all feel enthusiastic… Now let us enjoy tea and coffee in the natural environment."

"Yes," replied John with a relaxed smile.

"Sit relaxed, close your eyes and practice slow, effortless and deep breathing. Just observe your breath and continue relaxing. Find out which part of your body is not relaxed. Pay attention to it and relax it. Continue till you are totally relaxed. Focus your attention here and now. Now try to focus on 5 different sounds you hear and also on gaps between the sounds."

"Can you tell which different sounds you notice, Mitali?"

"I notice sound of my breathing and silence between two breaths, chirping of a group of birds passing by, sound of ducks from a bank of lake and snoring of John."

Everybody looked at John and laughed loudly. He was, by now, fully awoke.

"Sorry, I dozed during meditation."

"Do not worry, Mr. John. This generally happens while meditating," explained Vikas with a smile. "Now think about a past event, memory of which troubles you often and about the person who hurt you. Sincerely forgive that person and pray for his peace of mind. Picture the person standing in front of you."

Everybody followed the instructions.

"Make a list of all the persons you might have hurt and also those who might have hurt you. It is difficult, so be honest with yourself and take your time. After you have compiled your list, systematically go through each person on the list," explained Vikas. "Forgive yourself first. Once you forgive yourself, it's also important to clear the air with others. Apologize aloud to yourself stating, 'I forgive myself for hurting this person/those persons.' Relax and take a deep breath. You will instantly feel a sense of relief."

"In your mind's eye, explain to him how you felt then and now, and what happened during those hurtful times. After you have stated your views, let him acknowledge your pain. Watch his reaction and wait for his response," explained Vikas. "He will understand your point of view. Then hug him and tell that you forgave him. Release him from your troubled past and let your thoughts come back to the present."

"Face to face apology is best and most effective. If you can't bring yourself to ask for forgiveness in person, I still recommend telephoning or writing a letter of forgiveness."

"Then take up another such case and continue to forgive and forget. You will feel serenity and peace of mind within."

"What do you feel Reena?" asked Vikas. "Any comments?"

"The exercise is very effective. I had a grudge against a person. He had betrayed me earlier. I always felt uneasy thinking about him. Today I could effectively forgive him. I feel free and relieved. I have decided to talk to him on phone soon and convey my changed outlook to him," said Reena with a sigh of relief.

"That is appreciable." said Vikas. "Dr. Meena, do you also want to say something?"

"Yes Vikas, My step father created so many problems for me and he made my life miserable. I hated him all the time. Today I could analyze the situation with a positive mental attitude and forgave him totally. I am feeling totally relived today."

"Mitali, I find you that you are still stressed and uneasy. I watched frowns on your face. Is there any problem?" asked Vikas with concern. "May I help you Mitali?"

"I am successful in eliminating minor annoyances and antipathies today and during earlier workshops," asserted Mitali with traces of melancholy on her face. "I am not successful in forgiving one of my uncles. The hatred is of such an intensity, I cannot handle the situation alone. I totally failed to forgive him."

"I also realized this watching your expressions," said Vikas with a stoic face.

She looked gloomy and her eyes were still full of tears.

"I am sure, you are going to be successful this time," reassured Vikas with commiseration, putting his hand on her shoulder. "We will have one to one session very soon. Mr. John, I want to hear your experience."

"I rarely hate anybody. I rarely met a man to whom I did not like. I love all and hate none," squeaked john laughing aloud. "The exercise is, however, effective and I could eliminate a few minor grudges, I had with a few persons. This exercise will be useful in future also."

"Very good."

"I have another problem, which is personal in nature and it is not related to forgiveness," said John.

"Yes, you told me. That, we will take up in one-to-one session, sometime later."

"Thank you, Vikas," said John.

"Anybody wants to ask any question?"

Nobody budged.

"Now it is time to enjoy our lunch," suggested Vikas with a smile. "What do you think?"

"Yes," all squeaked in unison with a smile.

The steamy, hot and aromatic lunch was set on the table. Everybody enjoyed the delectable food. It was a wonderful experience to enjoy food in the open air together. The fresh cold breeze was soothing. Dr. Meena was taking her lunch oblivious of others presence. She did not notice when Vinod appeared from behind her.

"Hi beautiful," squeaked Vinod from behind and nudging the back of Meena with his fingers. "You are looking fresh and gorgeous, honey."

"Thanks Vinod. But restrain yourself, at least in presence of others," Dr. Meena blurted out with false annoyance.

"Please forgive me. I know you will not mind this time. We have to practice forgiveness."

"I will kill you, and then I will forgive myself," whispered Meena with a seductive smile. "How is the lunch?"

"Very tasty," said Vinod. "I hope, you also liked it. Should I bring anything for you?"

"Yes, it is tasty. It is a wonderful experience to take lunch in this environment." said Dr. Meena. "I have taken enough, thanks Vinod."

"I hope everybody is back. Now we are going to discuss how to live peaceful and stress free life," said Vikas. "Stress creates various problems in life. When there is stress, we can neither be peaceful nor happy."

"Can you give some tips to keep mind free from stress?" asked Mitali.

"Yes, I have a few valuable suggestions for you to soothe your nerves: Take 15 minutes nap... Merely lying down and taking rest can be equally restorative... Take a shower or a warm bath in a bath tub... Enjoy nature or go out to a park full of greenery and fragrant flowers... Listen to wind chimes, music, chirping of birds or rustling of leaves in the forest...Take time off for weekend outing to a natural place like this... Have fun and a sense of humor... get a massage... do something you love."

"How happiness is connected with peace," asked Shams curiously.

"Both are interlinked. You cannot be happy without peace of mind and you cannot be peaceful when you are sad," expounded Vikas. "But peace is more important than happiness."

"How?" asked Sofia. "Can you give an example?"

"Suppose someone dies in our families," elucidated Vikas. "We may remain serene and composed, if we accept the situation with faith, hope and love. People come and commiserate with us. We experience unconditional love of others who come to console us and share our grief. We are not happy, but we all feel peaceful in presence of God and loved ones."

"How can we be happy and free from stress?" asked John. "Please give me some more valuable tips."

"It is a very vast topic and volumes can be written on this topic," Vikas expatiated. "There are, however a few points, which you can keep in your mind to be happy and calm."

Everybody listened attentively. Their eyes lit up with curiosity.

"Everybody has his own definition of happiness. Some persons find happiness in getting success and getting their passionate desires fulfilled. For getting success you have to work harder and smarter and be a go-getter."

"What do you mean by 'go-getter'?" asked Shams.

"Simple… go out of your way to get what you want… to make an extra effort to achieve your passionate desire."

"Thanks for illuminating, Vikas," said Shams.

"Some people get real bliss in service of others," said Vikas. "They are happy, when they make others happy. They are go-givers."

"What do you mean by 'go-givers'?" asked Sofia interestedly.

"It means going out of way to give something to others, without any condition attached, to make them happy. It may be some gift, attention, knowledge, information and time which make them happy. This can be, going to them and giving a kind word, helping them, stopping your car at the crossroad to let people cross, giving your seat in a bus to someone else, or going and giving a small present to someone you love. The possibilities are infinite," Vikas explained. "When you make someone happy, you get inner peace and become happy, and at the same time, people also try to make you happy."

"The real happiness is achieved, when you make others happy. By helping others, you also get inner satisfaction and peace," Vikas added. "Helping others is like expressing gratitude to God. Bless everything and everyone you meet."

"A real go-giver plants a flower, which blooms in the garden of his own heart. He gives for the joy of giving, without expecting anything from others. He, very well, knows that respect for others does not admit of pretention and hypocrisy," said Vikas. "He never allows his left hand to know what his right hand does in charity, nor does he boast of his helpful attitude toward others."

"Please give me a few more tips to be peaceful and happy," requested Vinod. "I have always enjoyed adventurous life. Sometimes I feel that I want to be peaceful and blissful."

"It is a difficult question to answer," said Vikas. "But let us compile some points together: Always be appreciative and cheerful… Be helpful and thankful and reciprocate favors done to you… Affirm, 'I am now happy, joyful and better than millions.'… Sharing is important, as I told you earlier…. share love, joy and humor… Make others happy by helping and giving service to someone and do more than paid for," explained Vikas.

"Can you all suggest some more points? Let us brainstorm," said Vikas after a pause.

"Meditate, deep breathe, pray and relax to get immediate relief from stress," advised Meena. "Sleep is very important for release of stress."

"Can you suggest important tips to sleep better and releasing stress?" asked Sofia.

"Okay. For getting sound and relaxing sleep, avoid consuming sugar, caffeine or a heavy meal, just before you go to bed… Slow and rhythmic breathing would help you to relieve tension and fall asleep faster… Express eloquently without suppressing your feelings… If you feel the need to say something, say it… Opt for healthier eating alternatives… Avoid junk food completely or eat it in moderation," expatiated Dr. Meena in detail. "Here we have a few more tips to sleep better and faster. Listen to soothing music…You could even try aroma therapy… Bathing in tepid water, just before you go to sleep, will calm your senses and help you sleep better… Having a warm glass of milk is also helpful for sleep."

"I have a valuable suggestion for those who are prone to avoid sleeping either for work enjoyment," added Meena. "I am afraid that it is not easy to persuade you to alter a way of life, which you seem to have chosen, but benefits are enormous, if you do. Adhere to sleeping and getting up time. Bright light in the morning at a regular time should help you get up. If you fix time for sleeping and adhere to it, you will feel sleepy at the same time every night."

"Useful points for a relaxing sleep," said Vikas appreciating. "Thank you Dr. Meena. Sound, comfortable and relaxing sleep goes a long way to help us become stress-free. You have given us many valuable suggestions. Can you suggest a few more points for general stress release?"

"Okay. Opt for the scenic route, instead of the highway…
Exercise and walk in nature…spend more time regularly
with children, colleagues, friends and family members…
Get up early before sunrise and enjoy the serenity… You will
feel stress-free when you complete most of your important
work early in the morning… Do some small creative activity;
sketch, cook, stitch, sing and paint with loved ones… Always
make the most of time of well-deserved break," added Dr.
Meena. "Drink plenty of water instead of soft drinks and
other sugary drinks… Share humor and laugh loudly with
others. Laughter is the best medicine… Do not overwork
and take well deserved breaks between strenuous tasks."

"Thanks, Dr. Meena for so many valuable suggestions,"
uttered Vikas. "Your suggestions are appropriate and useful."

"Thanks, Vikas."

"Visualize positive outcomes during the day ahead and
set intentions of the day. Love yourself and make the choice
to remain cheerful," illuminated Mitali. "Write a note of
gratitude to someone who positively impacted your life.
Write 'thank you' notes often. Say something amusing to
people who help you."

"Marvelous suggestion, Mitali," said Vikas. "Now it is
your turn Reena."

"Meditate, deep breathe and relax. Take shower and
enjoy the feeling of warm water in the bath tub. Enjoy
massage, sauna and steam bath. Listen to your favorite music
and dance, as if nobody is watching you," Reena cooed with
her lips curled in a wonderful smile. "Look at pictures from
joyful occasions in your life and relish memory."

"Mr. John," Vikas prompted him for expressing his
views on the topic under discussion.

"Go out of your way to help others. Give an extra big
unexpected tip to the waiter. Say thanks to the attendant

who opens door for you. Give a loving hug to a person who never expected it from you. Say good morning and hello to new persons. Go out of your way to help a neighbor and an acquaintance," asserted John. "De-clutter and donate items, which you do not need. Invite friends to your house for a simple dinner. Do something for others and do not get found out."

"Very good points. You can compile your own list and not only compile but live that list," said Vikas. "You must believe that the happiness is achievable. You have attained it many times earlier. Others too have accomplished it. Realize that happiness does not arise from the acquiring physical or mental pleasure, but from the change of attitude, development of reason and live life according to decent values."

"I think we have discussed enough on this subject," Vikas added after a brief pause. "I am happy you all are interacting a lot. We are all enriched in many ways by these discussions."

Chapter-5

The sunlight of the rising sun was streaming into her window and inundating her room with mellow light when she woke early in the morning. It was impossible to experience dejection in that radiance. Reena sat up and listened to the birds still singing on the trees. The sound of movement and bustle of staff communicated her plainly that the day had already begun without her. She looked up for wall clock and noticed that it was already 6 o'clock.

She moved out for enjoying the fresh air and performing a daily gratitude walk. The air was pleasing and it was replete with the indescribable aroma of spring. The heavenly notes of bluebirds were audible from every side. Migratory robins were feeding in the orchard, whistling and calling out to their buddies.

Reena walked a few steps slowly, while expressing her gratitude to God at every step. The morning sun was shining in the clear sky, casting long shadows on the velvety grass, illuminating it with a golden light. She came back to go to swimming pool. Mitali, John and Vinod had already reached there and were swimming in the pool. She frolicked around in the swimming pool and swam to her heart's content. She enjoyed a lot swimming with everybody and later on talking and sipping the soft drink on poolside recliner.

She decided to spend her evening with Vikas. Reena had been naturally drawn to Vikas since the day she met him. Mitali had told her about Vikas on telephone. She had also advised her to deeply study his ideology and try to spend some time with him. She found him very motivating personality and she was always comfortable in his company. She was always eager to spend some time with him. At this age, he had, not only mastered noble success principles, but he was transplanting these wonderful ideas in others minds successfully. He was, not only putting them into practice regularly in his daily life, but also inspiring others to do so.

"What are you doing in the evening, Vikas?" asked Reena looking at him interestedly.

"Why, Reena," asked Vikas with a butter-soft voice. "May I help you?"

"To be frank, I was thinking about spending some time with you. I am feeling lonely today," said Reena. "Can we go for a walk in the evening?"

"I have some work to do relating to presentation. But, I am sure, it will not take much time and I can easily finish it sometime in the day, well before the evening," said Vikas with his usual smile. "We will go for a walk in the evening. Who wants to miss the company of gorgeous young lady like you?"

"Thanks, Vikas," mumbled Reena, unable to hide her excitement. She was delighted to hear his remark.

"It is my pleasure. I also wanted to share some moments with you. You impressed me a lot, when I met you that day," said Vikas with a charming smile. His pair of fond eyes noticed the amusement, which Reena experienced at the expected rendezvous. "You always looked so dazzling; it was difficult to remove my glance from you."

~~~~~~

He studied on laptop, updating the power-point slides. He, time to time, raised his eyes to look out at the open window and glanced at the fresh flowers in the vase on the table. He again started studying. He was joyfully smiling with delight in anticipation of the outing. Then there was a gentle rap on the door. Reena entered the room.

Reena was wearing a light blue track suit and walking shoes. She looked gorgeous. The mere sight of her, somehow, thrilled Vikas. Her deportment, beauty, politeness, along with her charming nature always caught his attention. She looked quite active and smart but a bit tired.

"How was your day? You look charming, though you seem to be a bit tired," asked Vikas. "I am ready and I was just waiting for you. Let us go."

"Yes, you are correct, may be it is because of today's hectic schedule," mumbled Reena with a feeble smile, walking hand in hand.

It was a delightful afternoon for a relaxing walk. The air was clear and cool but not actually uncomfortable. The ground beneath their feet was wet after the rain. There appeared only a few clouds in the sky, which gave no foreboding of rain in next few hours. Time to time, sun glimpsed to brighten the ambience. The floating cloud patches were forming exotic patterns in the sky. They strolled together with easy steps, clasping each other's hands for a long time under the chestnut-trees, loaded with fruits in their green shells. Reena loved this natural forest. It was so still, so gloomy, and so full of shadows and shades, a humid smell of wood, and tantalizing fragrance of spruce.

They had a wonderful time together walking. The birds had, by now, started returning to their nests. The sun was on the verge of setting and slanted rays were filtering through the foliage and were creating multihued patches of light.

"This blue track suit suits you and you look charming, Reena," Vikas squeaked, looking deep into her eyes. "Let us stroll a little more then we will sit on bench under that tree."

"Beautiful idea," cooed Reena with her usual charming smile. "I feel wonderful to amble here with you, in such beautiful natural surroundings."

"Yes, it is a magnificent experience to walk here with you," said Vikas. "I also like natural, peaceful and green forests. It is one of those serene, placid and peaceful evenings, in which God seems to come nearer to my soul."

They were enjoying the stroll together when they heard a rustle in the tree ahead. To their utter shock, a big snake fell down. She shrieked with horror to see quivering big snake in front of her. She felt a strong a feeling of trepidation. She was unable to overcome the feeling of dreadfulness. Frozen with horror, she was unable to move, feel or reflect for some time. She, at once became a quivering mass of cold flesh. She shuddered and became wet with perspiration. She struggled to recover her composure from internal convulsion to regain her poise. She felt relieved to see the snake move away towards nearby bushes.

He calmed her fear by putting his hand on her shoulder and comforted her by assuring, "Take it easy, Reena. You are a bold lady. All the snakes are not dangerous."

"But I have heard that all the snakes are venomous to some degree," said Reena.

"You are correct. All of them have venom, but most of them do not have enough of it to kill a human being. Most of them will never hurt you," said Vikas reassuringly. "Take, therefore, ample precaution, but never be scared to death like you are doing now."

"Thank you, Vikas for encouragement."

"I am here with you. Now relax and do not be afraid. You have seen that the snake has gone and disappeared in the bush. Let the fear also go and disappear. There is no reason to worry now," Vikas reassured to eliminate her fear.

"I also had also similar aversion for the snakes, but I was able to overcome the fear. I, later on, found that majority of them are harmless creatures. The only dangerously venomous species seen on our area are the rattlesnakes and the copperheads."

His words had soothing effect on her. Vestiges of horror, however, were still visible on her face. While trying to recover from paralyzing shock, she lost her equilibrium and slipped on a stone and stumbled. Fortunately Vikas was nearby and promptly extended his both hands to hold her. She was unhurt and safe in his arms. She almost hugged him and clasped him tight. She remained motionless and flaccid in his strong arms for some time. She slouched her head against his shoulder and her eyes closed out of utter exhaustion.

She felt euphoric in his arms. Overpowered by a sudden ecstasy, she was unable to breathe coherently. Vikas could easily feel the wild pounding of her heart against his own. He felt that the only sounds that broke the profound stillness of the solitary ambience were her wild heart beats and incoherent breath, as she came closer and closer.

"Walk carefully, lest you should fall," said Vikas with concern. "The path is narrow and full of slippery stones. How do you feel now?"

"I do not have to walk carefully when you are here to save me," said Reena with enchanting smile. "I am safe in your hands," she chuckled with an enigmatic smile after a pause. "I always feel comfortable in your presence. Thanks for this wonderful evening."

"You are welcome. I also had awesome time with you. You are a marvelous creation of God and a wonderful company," said Vikas.

"I have noticed that you have abnormal fear. This will hinder your personal growth, if you do not overcome it."

"Yes Vikas, I realize it, but I find myself helpless. Fearful thoughts enter my mind often unnoticed," said Reena. "Can you tell me how can I overcome it? I am generally obsessed with the feeling that something bad may happen."

"Be an optimist and have faith in God. He is always with you to help and guide you in the difficult moments. You might have noticed that most of the things we fear most never happen in life," assured Vikas. "When did you notice this extreme aversion for snakes for the first time?"

"It was in my childhood when I first time saw a big snake in my neighbor's house. It had bitten a child. It took lot of effort to save his life," delineated Reena after pondering for some time, recalling the incident. "The snake, however, was later killed by villagers."

"That morbid fear still lingers in your psyche, I suppose," said Vikas with concern. "Face the memory boldly. Study and learn facts and statistics about them. Then face actual snakes controlling your reaction. I am sure; you can easily overcome this morbid fear."

"Thank you Vikas for wonderful suggestions."

"Thoughts are only thoughts and treat them as such. They cannot harm you. Believe that they are for your help and safety."

"Thanks for practical and effective suggestions," said Reena thankfully. "Please suggest some more remedies for fear."

"Be vigilant and aware. When, next time fear knocks at your door, ask yourself; if such a thing ever happened to you earlier and what are the chances that this will happen now. May be the chance of not happening worst is more than chance of happening," Vikas expatiated in detail. "In justice to our own best interests, you should search every cranny of our heart and mind, lest you venture forth with any such weaknesses. There is no excuse, and we have no one to blame, if we allow any of them to journey along with us. Such fears we retain are excess baggage to be thrown away at the earliest opportunity."

"I think I lack requisite courage to go through this process," expressed Reena. "How can I have more courage, Vikas?"

"Reena; courage is what you require most to counter your abnormal fear. Courage is the best antidote to fear," explained Vikas. "Fear is illusory; it cannot live. Courage, on the other hand, is eternal and it will not die."

"How."

"Fortify your mind with optimism, courage and patience. Fortitude and presence of mind will sustain you through all dangers, just as a rock on the sea-shore stands firm and the waves do not affect it," explained Vikas. "A man who is endowed with courage is not affected by fear and he stands like a rock. Face fearful situations often with faith and courage. Do not lose track of thoughts when facing fearful situations."

"Thanks for motivation," said Reena. She was eager to learn more and her eyes were lit up with extreme curiosity. "Very interesting. Please tell me more in detail."

"Ponder over the advantages of courage and the disadvantages of fear. You will be motivated to overcome fear. Then taking an effective actions will be easier."

"Okay, I feel immensely motivated and inspired."

"Always remember that God is always with you and he never leaves you alone. He will bestow the requisite strength, fortitude and courage in face of fear. Identify yourself with the immortal fearless soul."

"That will certainly help a lot, Vikas," murmured Reena with lovely smile, continuing to consider him thoughtfully, as if not to miss any shade of meaning in what he said. "Prayers helped me a lot in eliminating fear in the past also. But I have found that our prayers are not answered all the time."

"These are always answered but in God's own time," explained Vikas. "We should ask for what we want, but we should be willing to accept what He gives. God always helps us, but he does it in his own way. Even if He does not give you what you want, do not worry. May be, he has better things in His mind. May be, time is not yet ripe for that. Have faith and be patient."

Looking at her wavering eyes, Vikas narrated a tale to make his point, 'One person was struck in high tides and his ship was destroyed. He saw the small island and cursed the God for misery. He, anyhow, erected a wooden house. One day lightning and thunder annihilated and burnt that too. He cursed God for that cataclysm also. Rescue team noticed smoke emanating from his burning wooden house and came to his rescue.' Only then he realized that God is always there to help, save and guide us in difficult moments."

"It is a magnificent motivational story, indeed."

"Have faith in God. He is always there to help you," said Vikas. "Live your life with vigor and don't let the fear of death close your options. Confidently venture into the life, which you have chosen to live."

"Be an optimist and always hope that something fantastic will happen today. Set intention of the day and visualize a splendid day ahead. Find more activities which give courage to fight fearful situations. Everything that tends to build up courage is an asset in life. The more we have of it the farther we go and the more interesting our lives becomes."

"Thank you Vikas for inspiring me to work on eliminating my fears," said Reena, her lips curled in a smile, looking deep into his eyes. She seemed to have regained her composure. He hugged her once more to comfort her and assuage her feelings. She returned hug spreading her arms and coming closer, but said nothing further in words. Her silence, however, conveyed a lot, and was more eloquent than the speech. She came so close that he could feel her warm breath on his face.

He reciprocated with a passionate hug. She put her head on his chest and took a deep breath. He lifted her chin and looked into her eyes. She also stared into his face, which was lit up with an uncanny smile, full of light with a profound gaze which was so curious and so exciting to him.

He became joyful, acutely and delightfully conscious of himself, of his own attractiveness to her. She looked so young, so gorgeous. She looked so dazzling; her glowing charm would easily have captivated a recluse.

"I am thankful to you my dear Vikas. You have given me so much happiness," Reena whispered. "It is a wonderful outing."

"I am also happy. You made my evening amazing," said Vikas. "I shall always relish the memory of beautiful moments shared with you."

"How can I reciprocate your loving gesture and wonderful hug?"

"Are you crazy? Continuous reciprocations may result in dangerous consequences," Vikas jested laughing and tried to change the topic. "I will always remember this brilliant evening with you. Thank you dear. I think we are getting late. Should we move now?"

"Yes. All will be waiting for us for dinner. Let us go and enjoy dinner together," mumbled Reena after a pause to catch her breath.

As Vikas anticipated, everybody was waiting for them for the dinner. As he entered, every face glowed with joy. They expressed happiness and welcomed them.

"Vikas, dinner is ready; and we are all waiting for you both. Where have you been this evening?" Mitali enquired.

"We had gone for evening walk together," interjected Reena with smile, entering the dining hall.

"Let us have dinner," suggested Sofia looking at every body with sweeping glance with a smile.

"What about dancing, before we proceed for dinner," Mitali chuckled. "We must create space for food."

"Wonderful idea," squeaked Vinod. "Come here everybody. Let us dance."

"Come Vikas and dance with me," chuckled Mitali with an enticing smile. She extended her hand toward Vikas. "It has been almost 2 years since the time we danced together in Bombay."

"Yes Mitali, You are correct. As at that time, even today, I am not an expert dancer," said Vikas hesitatingly with smile.

He accompanied her to the floor with alacrity. He galloped ahead, as if he was waiting for her invitation and went across to her, and gathered her like a beloved in his arms. She was so tenderly beautiful. Instinctively, she felt that he was desirous to dance with her.

Then the music commenced and everybody started dancing with alacrity. They were ecstatic and enjoyed dancing. The dance was animated and ecstatic.

Mitali danced and laughed with him with a boisterous merriment. Both danced energetically and joyfully, with his arms about her form. Her wondrous eyes, time to time, met his eyes seeking his, and then drifting again.

"You are a wonderful dancer and I will be your trainer today," Mitali chuckled with seductive smile, laughing with joy. "It is a wonderful experience to coach a handsome coach," she whispered in his ear with a soft voice. She was so careful that no third person could hear her words. This type of banter was new to him, but it amused him enormously. He scrupulously followed, as she guided him through complicated steps. Her movements were graceful yet sensual to such a degree that his pulse was pounding.

All of them were on the floor and danced for 20 minutes non-stop, till they were exhausted. All were enormously happy and danced together blissfully. Mitali, Reena, Shams and Vinod danced like expert dancers. They helped and guided others who could not dance well.

"I hope you liked the dance," asked Mitali.

"Yes, I enjoyed a lot and learned a few more steps," Vikas murmured with a butter-soft voice.

The dinner was already set on the tables. Everybody winded their way through the maze of gastronomic delights.

"Do you have any alcoholic beverages with dinner, like red wine?" asked John looking at Shams.

"I am sorry, Mr. John. There is no such arrangement," said Shams. "Mr. Vikas has not allowed us to do so."

"I have heard that red wine is beneficial for health," John mumbled softly, "if it is taken in moderate quantity."

"I do not agree with you Mr. John," retorted Shams.

"I also do not agree with you Mr. John," Vikas asserted, overhearing and interjecting. "It is harmful, even if you take moderate quantity, so as to make yourself cheery. When you are in a robust health, you may relish wine with seeming impunity, but you will notice its harmful effects after a few years of indulgence."

"Even if we take the moderate quantity of wine with the best food?" asked John.

"Yes Mr. John, you will suffer from its damaging effects on your health. You will, however, notice the damage only when it is already too late. Your health is the paramount blessing you enjoy. Without it, wealth, honors would be insipid, explained Vikas. "Its detrimental influence will blast the vigor of the strongest constitution. I suggest, therefore, that you should all take care of health. Without this asset other thing are bland."

"Thank you very much Vikas for a useful suggestion. I was misinformed. Now I know about its deleterious effects. I will always keep your suggestion in mind," John muttered. "But what beverage should I take?"

"Water, of course," retorted Vikas with smile. "While we are eating, water is the best beverage. You may take juice also, if you like, but the practice of drinking wine during dinner is hazardous."

"I have also heard that wine helps in the digestion of food," John muttered.

"Dr. Meena will educate you on this issue," said Vikas.

"You are correct, Vikas," Dr. Meena elaborated. "Consumption of wine in any quantity hardens food and renders it less digestible. Vikas has correctly explained."

"Thank you, Dr. Meena."

"While we are eating, water is the best beverage, as Mr. Vikas has explained to you," explained Dr. Meena with a bright smile, pouring water in his glass. "Here it is to your health and happiness."

"The custom of drinking fermented liquors, and particularly wine, during dinner, is a very pernicious one. The idea that it assists digestion is false," expatiated Dr. Meena further.

"Some people say that taking water during meals should be avoided," interjected John.

"Mr. John you will agree that we should take plenty of water during the day. It cleanses our body and keeps us healthy. If you want to avoid intake of water during meals, take it before meals and after meals," said Vikas. "Sometimes, you may add small quantities of sugary drinks and juices to make meals more palatable."

"Thank you, Mr. Vikas," muttered John. "Thank you, Dr. Meena for educating us on the subject."

"Thank you, Dr. Meena for your valuable suggestions. Thank you Mr. John for making discussion interesting and lively," said Vikas. "We should develop our mind and personality, at the same time we should maintain sound health. The prime necessity of life is health. But if we do not make use of this good health, it will waste itself away and never come back. It often disappears entirely due to lack of interest on the part of its thoughtless owner."

"Developing our body without nurturing our soul will create feeling of emptiness. We should keep trilogy of our endowments; mind, body and soul, in magnificent condition," added Vikas. "When you direct your energies to unlock full potential of these three endowments, you enjoy the real joy. Like the steam engine, we are keeping the fires going by exercise, wholesome thinking and sincerity of purpose. We are the engineers. Our hand is on the throttle."

"Doing the proper exercise, looking wholesomely upon life, believing in ourselves, are all parts of the wise practice, which leads to success, happiness and peace. Exercise is important for good health and walking is an important exercise."

"Get ready, therefore, tomorrow and reach central hall. We all will go together for a morning walk from there. Please put on dresses and shoes which are suitable for jogging," said Vikas after dinner.

"Where will we go?" asked Dr. Meena curiously.

"We are going to a nearby verdant park with lots of greenery with fragrant flowers galore," said Vikas. "We will go by car. It is 10 minute drive through the lush green dense forest."

Chapter-6

It was a beautiful and luxuriant park, replete with plenty of fragrant flowers. An open and beautiful spot was surrounded by thick forest from three sides and on fourth side there was an attractive small lake. Location of the park situated on the bank of the lake was stunning.

The cold breeze filtered through the trees and the bushes in the forest, was inundating the park and refreshing everybody with heavenly olfactory delight. The sun was shining brilliantly when they reached there.

On the other side of the lake, there were steep hills. The lake, abounding with lotuses, looked amazing. In the lake various water birds were frolicking around. Cold breeze was blowing, brushing hairs and caressing cheeks. It was a wonderful experience to be in the park.

"Let us first stroll around this beautiful spot. Take your own time, as there is no hurry. We are going to stay for the whole day in this exotic natural setting. Do some flexing and stretching exercises, which you normally do. They will loosen your muscles and joints and increase blood circulation," Vikas advised.

"I do not do any exercise except jumping to conclusions nowadays," Mitali jested smiling. "Please guide me."

"Dr. Meena will help you," said Vikas smiling. "Everybody, please help others also. After that just walk, move around, enjoy and relax. Feel free to do whatever you like."

"How do you feel Dr. Meena?" asked Vikas smiling. "I hope you like this place."

"I feel marvelous. It is a wonderful experience to walk with all in this exquisite natural ambience," chuckled Meena with a smile. "We rarely get such an opportunity in the cities. We live there at a frenzied pace, away from nature."

"Attention here and now! Everybody, please come here and sit down on the grass, cross legged…" said Vikas. "Relax a bit and breathe slowly and normally… Close your eyes… Do not try to alter your breathing for a few seconds… Take a relaxed, slow but deep breath…Just breathe normally and naturally with an effortless ease… Be aware of your breathing and focus attention on inflow and outflow of rhythmic breathing… If attention drifts, bring it back gently in the moment… Listen to the air moving into your body and feel your lungs swell…"

Vikas sat cross legged and expatiated in detail, so that everyone could understand. Everybody followed his instructions.

"Observe the up and down movement of your belly… Breathe out slowly… but completely… through your mouth… let the air escape on its own… While doing it, be aware of inner body and feel energy in every part of your body," said Vikas with a slow pace and soft and controlled voice. He also guided others. "Keep your eyes closed and… count your blessings… Think about the things and amenities you are grateful for… Just ponder… there are so many things… You have free clean air to breath, clean water to drink, money to share and spend, good health and a wonderful mind in a wonderful body."

"Now feel relaxed within. All tension has evaporated. It is such a wonderful feeling in wonderful place," Vinod mumbled. "I think it will be beneficial, if we share our experiences and ideas with each other."

"Brilliant suggestion, Vinod. You may all share your ideas with each other," said Vikas. "Speak loudly so that everybody can hear. Dr. Meena, do you want to share something?"

"I feel relaxed and placid as an unruffled lake, tranquil within. Relaxing and breathing in such a magnificent environment is a delightful experience. I am filled with peace and gratitude," said Meena.

"Can you share your real life experience about gratitude?" asked Vikas.

"In my nursing home, I had a terminally ill patient under my treatment. One day one of his relatives visited the hospital and remarked, 'How does it feel to think that you are going to die very soon?' She was first shocked to hear such a gratuitous remark, but soon regained her usual serenity. She smiled and said with a glow on her face, *'I have gracefully accepted the fact that we are all going to die today, tomorrow or some other day and turn into dust. This is a fact and you cannot deny, can you? In the life of humanity one hour, one day, one year and 20 years do not make much difference. We have to be and must be happy in every moment. We should live a wonderful life and always be grateful to God. I wake up every day with unlimited enthusiasm. I bless everything and everybody. I express gratitude to God for giving me another magnificent day.'* I was inspired and impressed by her positive attitude and gratefulness," Dr. Meena expounded.

"It is a wonderful example of grateful attitude. Thanks Dr. Meena," said Vikas appreciating. "Now we will do gratitude walk."

"What is that?" queried Sofia with a smile.

"Come here everybody and stand relaxed together… Take a few deep breaths… Think about something, for which you are grateful to God… Fill your mind with gratitude… Let your mind be inundated with gratefulness… There are so many things to be grateful for… You have wonderful friends… You have sound health… You woke up alive today healthy…" said Vikas.

"Start walking slowly in a relaxed manner with easy steps with focused awareness in this moment… Be focused and present with one hundred percent of yourself. Observe how you are breathing in and breathing out. Keep your body relaxed," Vikas explained further. "You have so many blessings and things in your mind, for which you are grateful to God. While walking, repeat them in your mind, at every step. At every step, count a blessing and express your gratefulness to God. Do it continuously for 20 minutes and do not think about anything else. If your awareness drifts, bring it softly back in the moment."

"I cannot walk, as I am feeling pain in my left leg," said Reena, looking at Vikas with a grim face.

"Do not worry, Reena. I will help you," said Vikas with a concern. "Take two slow step, breathing in, saying 'in, in'. Then take two slow steps, breathing out, and uttering 'out, out'. If you still feel pain, then take slower steps, one step while inhaling and one step while exhaling. Continue only so long as you feel comfortable."

"Thanks Vikas, I can now manage it," said Reena with a mild smile.

All walked slowly on the lush green grass for half an hour in a relaxed manner with full concentration. They were so much engrossed in their activity that nobody looked at each other.

"How did you like gratitude walk?" asked Vikas.

"It is wonderful, refreshing and relaxing," said Mitali. "I feel now terrific after doing it. My mind is filled with gratitude. I will like to share something about my experience with gratitude and inner joy associated with it."

"Very good, please go ahead," Vikas prompted, encouraging her to express. "Go ahead."

"Once I decided to express my gratitude to God daily. I concentrated more on what I have. I found that there are so many blessings, which God has given me. I, sometimes, wrote them on a paper. I practiced gratitude walk daily in the morning," said Mitali. "I paid attention on what I already have; also on what I want and worked for it. I visualized getting it and I gave thanks to God in advance."

Everybody listened with interest.

"I blessed everything and everybody. When you pay attention on something it grows and expands. I realized that I have so many things, which many persons do not have," she continued. "I watched daily for a few minutes 'The secret', a terrific movie. This motivational movie inspired me further to be grateful to God and have a positive mental attitude. By practicing all these things, I found that people with whom I interacted became even more kind to me."

"Wonderful example, Mitali."

"Now my work and mundane activities appear easy and more pleasant. I have, now, more time to do what I need to do. Friends are now coming forward to help me. I got plenty of rewards maintaining inner joy and serenity," added Mitali.

"Thanks for sharing your magnificent experience," said Vikas. "It is very inspiring indeed."

"We have discussed enough about gratitude walk. Now, we will discuss and practice power walk. It is very useful for health," said Vikas. "Without robust physique and sound health, all other things are insipid. A man, therefore, needs first of all to build upon his physique. Regular exercise, should be the first thing on his program. Play games and do different type of exercises to keep your body rejuvenated. Practice deep breathing, take plenty of fresh air in a natural surrounding and enjoy long power walks. Even a short 10-minute power walk alone or with your partner can work wonders in overcoming state of laziness," elaborated Vikas.

"How is it different from fast walking and jogging?" asked Sofia.

"Power walking is a cross between regular walking and jogging. For power walk you require running shoes, this is why I had asked you to come in running shoes."

"Why?" asked John.

"Running shoes flex most at the ball of the foot. Since feet swell while walking, shoes should allow for that extra space."

"Okay."

"Do not we require warm up before we start?" asked Meena.

"Good question, Dr. Meena. We require warm up before we start," said Vikas. "It is advisable to do some stretching exercises for a few seconds, before we actually start power walking. Stretching helps warm the body up prior to exercise and power walk. It is the perfect antidote for long periods of stillness and immobility. It is an important part of any exercise program. We must do a few stretching exercises, now in this moment."

"Lovely suggestion, Vikas. Stretching body works wonders for rejuvenation also," added Meena. "The body becomes warmer and more flexible."

"Yes Dr. Meena, it is invigorating too," explained Vikas. "Now stand up straight, without bowing your back or leaning forward. Holding your core straight will help your muscles work together and augment your walking speed," instructed Vikas. "Look ahead, not down, and focus on a point about 20 feet in front of you."

"Hold your head high, with chin parallel to the ground, to avoid neck pain. Relax your shoulders," delineated Vikas demonstrating. "Hold your abdominal muscles firm. Bend your elbows to about 90 degrees. Keep them close to your body. Allow your hands to relax in a slightly curled position."

"Next time, you may carry either an I-Pod or a mobile with inspirational recordings to listen. You may simply enjoy the sounds of nature, as you raise your heart rate and expand your lungs. Stretching, meditation and deep breathing in the park, along with vigorous walking, revitalize body and mind," said Vikas. "Swing your arms forward, alternating with your steps."

"How far should we swing our arms?" asked Meena.

"Your hands should not cross your chest. Roll your feet as you walk. Stride forward with one foot, your heel striking the ground first. Roll your foot forward and push off with your toes. Bring your other foot forward, just as you are pushing off with the toes of the front foot," Vikas explained further. "I hope all of you have properly understood?"

All nodded affirmatively in unison.

"Now go ahead and start walking," instructed Vikas. "Continue walking for a few minutes."

"Everybody walked vigorously for approximately 10 minutes."

"You all might be tired by now. Please take rest, then we will take lunch," assured Vikas with a smile. "You may take lunch in groups or alone, in open or behind the verdant buses with fragrant flowers. The waiters will set your tables according to your choice. Choose your partners, if you want to take your lunch in a group."

Vinod and Dr. Meena requested the waiter to set their table in a solitary place, behind tall ferns, where they would not be disturbed. They relished tempting lunch, looking at each other with loving glances. Time to time, she raised her glances to lovingly look at him warmheartedly. She kept her eyes on him except when he looked toward her, and then she instantly turned away her gaze.

"Lovely food with a gorgeous friend," squeaked Vinod with smile. "I will never forget this moment."

"I am also on top of the hill," squeaked Meena with seductive smile. "Lunch is also tasty."

"Try this," squeaked Vinod putting a morsel of pomfret piece in her mouth dipping in a sauce.

"Thanks Vinod, I have already tasted it. It is quite delectable and its aroma is magnificent." she reciprocated putting a morsel in his mouth, smiling lovingly at him with a charming smile. "Taste this sweet from my hand."

"How was the lunch?" asked Vikas. "I hope all of you enjoyed it."

"It was wonderful," cooed Reena. "Food was very tasty. There were so many varieties."

"I will now discuss 'Unconditional Love'," said Vikas. "Unconditional love is real love."

"What do you exactly mean by an unconditional love?" asked Mitali.

"It is love without any condition attached."

"I do not think it is possible to love someone, without any condition attached, regardless of what they do, behave or say, without accompanying sense resentment," said Sofia, "as we experience daily in family life."

"Have you not received such love from your mother and from father? They are also in family," retorted Vikas. "Okay, I will let you know. First you tell me Sofia, what do you mean by unconditional love?"

"Unconditional love means to me: I get butterflies in my stomach, when I think about him. I love him, regardless of how he may treat me. I love him, even if numerous other guys have crush on me," delineated Sofia with a charming smile. "I miss him so much, even if he does not care for me. When all I can think about is kissing him, hugging him and being with him, although he is out of country and away in some distant land."

"Who is that lucky guy?" asked John laughing loudly. Everybody laughed joyfully in unison.

"I have yet to find out," Sofia retorted.

"May be, you have already found and you are not telling us," chuckled Vinod laughing.

"You never know," Sofia retorted with an enigmatic smile.

"May be it is you, handsome," Mitali interjected, looking at Vinod, joyfully.

"Thanks," Vinod mumbled, blushing profusely. Everybody laughed joyously, relishing the banter.

"Now allow me to share my views on what unconditional love is. You have unconditional love when you love everyone and everything without attaching strings and without judging them," Vikas expounded. "It is made up of three unconditional properties in equal measure; acceptance, understanding and appreciation."

"How to develop such a love?" asked Sofia.

"Have a sincere esteem, adoration and reverence for the people you encounter. Always treat them as equals;

not inferiors or superiors in any way," expounded Vikas. "Practice it in everyday life, at every opportunity."

"Unconditional love is enormously soothing; physically, mentally and emotionally and it is a powerful medication for today's stress," expatiated Vikas. "An abundance of love, especially unconditional love, will restore the beauty contained in every moment. What do you think, Dr. Meena?"

"Yes, Mr. Vikas," asserted Meena with her usual composure. "All humans need touch and love for them to prosper, especially during childhood. For babies, love and touch are indispensable, as they cannot grow properly without these loving gestures. Unconditional love and touch provide a very special kind of nourishment for all age groups."

"Thanks, Dr. Meena," said Vikas. "As you have delineated, even as an adult, your body needs to be touched. It is the most basic need of all human beings. Shams, can you give an example of such a love, in which no condition was attached?"

"Once I was standing in a flower shop, where a man was holding a dozen roses in his hand. When he reached the cashier's counter, he realized that the cashier looked depressed. The man smiled lovingly at him and squeaked, 'I am buying 11 of these roses for my wife and this 12th rose is for you. I have selected it for you. I hope you will like it.' And then, he handed over to the cashier the 12th rose. The cashier was astounded for this gesture and reciprocated with an appreciative smile," Shams narrated. "Everybody standing there was happy to see this lovely reciprocation."

"Very appropriate example, Shams. We should take the first step to go and give; and begin to share our love without expecting anything in return. When we bring unconditional love into our personal, professional, community and family lives, we initiate bringing back real happiness to our lives," elaborated Vinod in detail. "Express your love everywhere without any condition attached. If you love someone unconditionally, you do not judge, blame or find him bad. You create an amiable environment."

"Do not you have some practical exercise or game for this practice?" asked Mitali with a smile.

"Thanks for reminding me, Mitali. Here we will do a small exercise, before boredom creeps in," chuckled Vikas with a smile. "Please stand up and choose a random partner. Stand relaxed and decide among yourselves who is 'A' and who 'B' is."

Mitali and John were in one group and Vinod and Dr. Meena were in another group. Both the pairs were standing in close proximity. Shams stood with Sofia and Reena was alone so she inched towards Vikas.

"All the pairs please hug your partners," instructed Vikas, smiling, noting hesitation. "Do not hesitate please… Go ahead… You will not lose anything… You all will feel wonderful."

"Angel hug or tight hug?" Reena squeaked in a jubilant mood, with laughter.

"Obviously, angel hug, for our comfort and safety," shot back Vikas laughing hilariously. Everybody laughed. "Our ribs are valuable parts of body."

"All 'A's will say to 'B's, "I love you my dearest friend…as you are…sincerely…without expecting anything from you… without any condition attached… now… in this moment… from core of my heart," elucidated Vikas. "Repeat it three times with feeling… as if you mean it."

"Now all 'A' and 'B' will reverse the roles and repeat those words 3 times as earlier. You may repeat the exercise a few times more, looking deep into eyes of each other with emotion and feeling."

"I love you my dearest friend… as you are… sincerely… without expecting anything from you… without any condition attached… now… in this moment… from core of my heart," Vinod mumbled with a butter-soft whisper. He repeated 3 times with slow pace, looking deep into her eyes. She was feeling uneasy when Vinod constantly uttered these words with constant gaze.

"Really?" asked Meena curiously with a dim voice.

"Do not act funny. We are doing exercise in a workshop," said Vinod. "Repeat the same sentence 3 times, looking deep into my eyes."

"I love you my dearest friend… as you are… sincerely… without expecting anything from you… without any condition attached… now… in this moment… from core of my heart," Dr. Meena whispered with an enigmatic smile tightening the hug carefully, so that nobody could notice. "My sweetheart, it is not simply an assertion, I mean it."

They were jolted out of their trance when they heard voice of Vikas.

"Let us now share our experiences," advised Vikas. "Do you want to share something, Mr. Shams?"

"Hugging is a wonderful and much neglected behavior. It is most effective stress reliever. We require more of it in our life. We must hug more often," affirmed Shams. "This hug reminded me the situation when my cousin was going to live in the hostel in Bangalore. It had a soothing effect on my tension ridden psyches. Tears came to my eyes, but now I have regained my serenity and feel immensely relieved. Uttering those words you told me have profound effect. Now I understand the importance of hug. I also realize, what unconditional love is."

"Great." cooed Vikas. "Anybody else wants to share his experiences?"

"As a Doctor, I have experienced unconditional love on various occasions. Hugging is a wonderful way to express that. Hugging has tremendous effect on growing children and adults alike. There should be more hugging in almost all relationships," asserted Meena. "My mother used to hug me often, whenever she realized that I was not comfortable. My father, however, rarely hugged me. Positive assertions about unconditional love have marvelous effect."

"Wonderful. Take initiative to start hugging your father also, when you go back," said Vikas. "It is never too late. He will reciprocate your gesture with the same affection. Mr. John, do you want to share something?"

"Yes Mr. Vikas, I want to share an incident from my own life," said John. "I was sitting in a train with my girlfriend. One young lady, who had come to see her parents off, was there in the train. She was looking at me, as if trying to recall something. My girlfriend was also looking at her and me, time to time, suspiciously. The young lady stood up impulsively and hugged me with a charming smile, oblivious of others presence. Her parents and my girlfriend were stunned, so was I. Before we could react, she said, 'You are Mr. John, I suppose. You are the person who saved my life, one year before.' Then, I also remembered the incident, she was referring to."

Then she turned towards her parents and said, "Do you remember the incident, I told you, dad?"

"Yes dear, you had fallen down on railway line and he jumped and pulled you aside to save you from an approaching train. Thank you my dear son," said her father, standing up and hugging me. "Helpful persons like you have made this planet wonderful. God bless you."

"Very good example, John," said Vikas. "You are a benevolent person with a helpful attitude. You are a marvelous creation of God. There is, was, have been or will be no one in this world like you."

"I have one more episode to share."

"Please go ahead," Vikas encouraged him to speak.

"Wife of a friend of mine was hospitalized for a long time for a rare disease. She was required to remain in the hospital. My friend got himself admitted in the hospital, just to remain with her all the time. He helped her, took meals with her," said John. "She has now regained her health and both are living a magnificent life happily, together. They are living example of an unconditional love."

"Thanks for sharing, Mr. John."

"I also want to share an episode," muttered Shams.

"Please go ahead," said Vikas encouraging him.

"An army soldier in a thick forest heard an agonizing voice from a fellow soldier from behind. He sought permission from the commander to go back and give a helping hand to his colleague and close friend. But he refused to grant the permission, fearing the risk of his life. The soldier pleaded incessantly, till he was allowed to go back to help him against wishes of the commanding officer. He came back and informed the officer, 'Sir, He is dead.' 'I told you not to take risk to go back. You could have lost your life also. I do not want to lose a wonderful soldier like you. Was it not a mistake to go back?' Soldier replied with tears in his eyes, 'Officer, it was not a mistake. When I reached there, he was still alive and his last words were, 'Dear friend, I knew you would certainly come back. In fact I was waiting for you. Now I can die comfortably and peacefully. You fulfilled my last wish. Go back my dearest friend, live your dreams, be happy. God bless you and your family members.' I am happy I took the risk and went back."

"Very touching story, indeed!" exclaimed Sofia with sad voice and tears in her eyes. "You cannot live your dream at the expense of others. People, who do so, are unscrupulous. We need to love unconditionally and make personal sacrifices for our family, colleagues, friends, and those we care about and who depend on us."

"Marvelous example, very touching story, indeed," said Vikas.

"How can we develop such an unconditional love?" asked John.

"Have a passionate desire to develop such a trait in your personality. Take an initiative to start a chain reaction," said Vikas. "Make a new friend and help him without condition. Give for the joy of giving, without expecting anything in return. Bless and thank everything and everyone. Be grateful to God for His enormous blessings. Give someone a compliment and do a random act of kindness without being found out."

Chapter-7

Mitali opened a glamour magazine to flip through, while relaxing on bed and calming herself down. Almost everybody had planned to go for an outing next day, but she opted to stay in her suite to sleep and relax. She chose to remain in absolute seclusion after the hectic schedule. Reading, while lying relaxed in the bed, played its soporific magic and very soon she felt drowsy.

She fell quickly into a sound sleep. She was awakened early in the morning by a subdued rap at the door blended with chirping of birds on nearby trees. It was still a bit dark and quiet. The knock was incessant and patiently persistent. She got up reluctantly rubbing her eyes and opened the door.

"What are you doing sweetie? Are you still enjoying romantic dreams?" squeaked Reena, coming inside the room and hugging her tight. "You are not going for an outing that is okay, but you can at least take breakfast with us."

"Okay, I will be there and have breakfast with you," said Mitali, still rubbing softly her eyes and yawning. "But why did you wake me up so early?"

"Because, according to Benjamin Franklin: *'Early to bed and early to rise, makes a man healthy, wealthy and wise.'*"

"An age-old saying, Is not it?" asked Mitali smiling, "and I am not a man, but a woman, who is yet to find out a suitable man for her who is 'healthy, wealthy and wise'.

"Have patience dear. Time may not yet be right. If winter comes, spring cannot be far behind."

"Thanks dear," said Mitali.

"There are so many benefits of rising early in the morning. It is not merely a saying, it works in daily life. We get an opportunity of greeting a wonderful new day, hearing the birds chirping. We get an ample time to say thanks for our blessings. It also gives us time to exercise. You can easily go for a jog, do a few laps in the pool, take sauna and steam bath, practice yoga or hit the gym with plenty of time at hand. We have all these facilities here in this resort. Of course, there is nothing like beginning the day with a dose of meditation. It will help calm your mind and sharpen your reflexes to keep you going through your busy schedule of work."

"Thank you very much for beautiful guidance," said Mitali with a smile. "Tell about yourself. How was your night, dear? Let us talk over a cup of tea."

"I had the most wonderful and rejuvenating sleep. I am relishing every moment of my stay on this island," said Reena, "that too with you."

Both were always happy together and spent maximum time in company of each other, whenever they had an opportunity. Strange and inviolable intimacy had existed between them for a long time. While they chatted intimately, the waiter brought and poured out for them steamy, aromatic and delicious tea. Reena sighed in delight as she took her first sip, leaning on the luxurious back of leather sofa.

"I hope you are also having wonderful time on this resort," cooed Reena.

"Yes Reena," said Mitali, "and I am thankful to you for attending this workshop and giving me a wonderful company."

"Thanks for the tea, Reena. I will wait for you in the dining hall."

Mitali took shower and did breathing and yogic exercise, till she started feeling drowsy again. She slept again for some time. She woke up this time totally relaxed and rejuvenated.

A feeling of nostalgia crept in her mind. She realized that her reverie was leading to despondency. She rose, shook herself, and strode toward the window and opened it. The brilliant slanting sunshine poured in through the window. She looked out of the window and noticed to her utter delight that the grass was wet and green. In the meant time a few white birds with black traces alighted on a tree nearby and poured out a jubilant song. For a few moments the joy, that had been almost dead in her heart temporarily, revived. She looked appreciatively at the bird, blessing it in her heart for the lovely song.

She got fresh and got ready. Her reflections were interrupted by a noise at the door, which was scarcely audible. She again heard a gentle rap on the door, as if somebody was knocking intermittently. She stood up and opened the door.

"Are you ready?" asked Reena entering inside.

"Almost. Come inside Reena and sit down," said Mitali. "I will be ready fast… please, give me a minute."

Everybody was in a holiday mood and ready to utilize time in their own way. All were in jubilant mood and were busy in planning their trips.

Mitali took baked fish, omelet and juice and came to sofa, where John was sitting alone. John appeared to be restless and his head was buried in his hands. He appeared to have sunk into the depths of nostalgia. He was muttering something to himself, as lonely people sometimes do. Then he raised his head a bit and stared pensively in the distance. He drew in the breath, which was decidedly unsteady. He was jolted out of despondency, when he felt that someone was standing near him. Raising his glance suddenly, he saw Mitali standing in front of him, smiling with her usual charm.

"Are you okay?" Mitali mumbled, breaking the cycle of his thoughts. "Why do you look so gloomy and where is your breakfast? Are you not planning to go out?"

"I have no company, so I have decided to remain here, in absolute solitude and relax," said John jolting out of listlessness. He had been brooding and suffering from uneasiness since morning, which had become, by now, more pronounced. A faint color came into his face, and he looked positively happy, as she sat down near him, with her breakfast plate in her hand. Her conversation tranquillized and comforted him a lot.

"I was also planning to remain here, but now I feel fresh and feel like going out," chuckled Mitali with a charming smile that was totally mischievous. "If you do not mind, we can go out together. Stop feeling miserable, anymore. Stop all brooding, nostalgia and looking at reminiscences. Come and make new ones with me."

"That is a wonderful idea… Yes… We will go out together." Thanks Mitali," squeaked John with jubilation. He felt an instant delight to hear her invitation. "Where should we go?"

"There is a magnificent spot on nearby hills. It will take only 40 minutes to reach there by car. You will enjoy the long drive through hilly jungles and trekking on the hills."

Both were extremely happy together. Both sneaked glances to look at each other, time to time. John was elegantly dressed and looked pretty smart.

The road was full of difficult slopes and sharp turns, but John drove adroitly, confidently and fearlessly. He appeared to be happy and in the pink of condition. They felt, as if they were passing into a kind of dream world, liberated from the conditions of actuality. The journey was exquisite. He happily drove along the serpentine road in the midst of the verdant thick forest. Patches of sunlight, filtering through huge trees, looked stunning. As they ascended and approached seemingly green hills, they found only a few trees on the brilliantly glistening land.

Regardless of the outer glory, Mitali's heart was focused upon John. The distance proved less than they had imagined. They had to cross the valley ahead to ascend the summit. Still, eager to reach the peak, they pushed on. The sun, by now, had gained height to put forth its supremacy, but its effect was, to some extent, mitigated by the pleasant cold breeze. Ultimately they reached the pinnacle, which they were aiming at.

The view was fantabulous. They were happy and realized that the place was replete with natural beauty. It was a wonderful experience to be on that spot. An excellent view stretched in all the directions.

There was peculiar movement of breeze in these strange elevations, where earth and clouds appeared to meet. At these higher altitudes, the character of the forest had changed significantly. Now, the trees were not pines, but firs and spruce, which were relatively thinner and taller.

They felt ecstatic, walking together, hand in hand. The fast breeze came whistling down with sand and pebbles. As they steadily and slowly climbed higher and higher, the view become more exquisite and the breeze became faster, frostier and chillier.

"Wow, lovely!" exclaimed Mitali, climbing slowly, holding John's hand firmly in her hand. Her personal consciousness was almost lost in the intense joy, which the ambience had aroused in her. They had wonderful time walking, climbing and frolicking around joyfully. He had peculiar feeling to walk and interact with her. She too looked very happy and joyful.

She looked so gorgeous that it was difficult for John to remove his glances from her. He smiled looking deep into her eyes. She put her hand over her mouth to hide the smile she could not prevent from coming to her attractive lips.

John observed, to his utter delight, that she had sharp pointed features accentuated by pinkish skin texture. What stood out was her overtly seductive and sexy sense of style. She looked charming and glamorous. She felt inner joy to notice that he was constantly looking at her with fond eyes.

He had not realized that she had started breaking down the armor around John's heart. She was in a jubilant mood. He looked up into laughter of her eyes and the joy on her face. Subjugated by his desire, he slipped his arm softly around her waist, and drew her closer to him, while walking. Awfully, shocks ran over her body, like shocks of electricity, as if many volts of electricity suddenly struck her down. Stunned, her heart almost fainted, but she soon regained her composure. She was now becoming braver and welcoming what was happening between them.

As his arm was strong to balance her safely on difficult ascending slope, she acquiesced under its secure grasp. He seemed to gather her, her love and her beauty into himself avidly.

She looked at him with her dazzling eyes that seemed to have undergone some metamorphosis. She was feeling relaxed and comfortable. She seemed to melt and to flow into him, as after some feeble wavering, her arms also came around his neck. They hugged each other for a pretty long time.

They were jolted out of their dreamy state by a peculiar crashing sound. At the same time, they also experienced a mild tremors of the ground under their feet. To their dismay, they noticed that earth had been loosened far up the hillside and was coming down in the perfect torrent. John ran to a safer spot, holding firmly the Mitali's hand, but she slipped and stumbled. She was dismayed, noticing the unforeseen occurrence.

He helped her to her feet, holding her hand. One small pointed stone fell on her shoulder and she screamed with unbearable agony. An icy emotion appeared on her usually placid face. She could not lift one of her hands and all of her body started shaking and quivering spasmodically. She sat in an anguish which affected her every feature. She made gasping sound as her breathing steadied. As tears subsided, she started shuddering in the aftermath.

"Are you okay, Mitali?" asked john holding her with both hands with tenderness and sympathy that expressed itself in his touch. She was too confused to be conscious of herself. She came very close to him under a huge rock. Stone pieces were still falling in torrent, but they were feeling safe under the rock. She was upset and terrified and he could feel her wild heart beats. A trail of gentle melancholy lay over them.

They were yet to recover from this impending calamity, when they observed that some quivering object was hanging from the edge of the cliff nearby. Out of this they saw emerging a brownish glistening object. It came slowly forth and fell down in front of them at a short distance. They shuddered with dismay to realize that it was nothing but a gigantic snake with a strange flat head like a spade. It was motionless for a few moments and then raised its head, wavered and quivered with frenzied movement. Then after some time, to their relief, it moved slowly away, creeping on a downward slope.

Then the silence ensued, except for a few desultory words spoken by john to console Mitali. They were too astounded to speak for some time. They just stood there staring in amazement, fraught with poignant fear. Mitali clung to John. He gazed into her whitening face and hugged again to comfort her. He rubbed his hand on her hand, arm and bruised shoulder, softly, for some time. He noticed that tears sprang to her eyes. An anguish and a crushing exhaustion overwhelmed her and made her wobbly.

John seemed completely overawed by the tempest of her anguish. She felt an excruciating pain, but she retained her senses, and tried to divert her thoughts by watching John who was trying his best to help her. They had not foreseen the dreadful incident that had happened to them.

They, anyhow, managed to walk slowly. They calmed their breath by relaxing and slowing down the speed further. John took out his handkerchief and wiped softly her streaming eyes. Mitali still experienced an excruciating pain in her body. Every bone in her body ached so maliciously that she could hardly drag herself along. She could, neither complain, nor scream. Whatever strength she had at her disposal, she was utilizing for carrying her own load.

John's equanimity, serenity and considerate voice gave her sufficient solace. He looked at her openly, lovingly and compassionately. A ray of hope shot into her dark eyes and the gleam of a smile began to show through her anguish. Now the delightful sparkle played in the depths of his transparent eyes. She was experiencing an unusual joy in his loving gestures.

The wind had, by now, subsided considerably and the sky was clear, except for a few patches of clouds here and there. They stood aside, motionless, as if a little astounded, as they looked at the cliff above. Its magnificence was not affected by the storm and it still looked wonderful. At the base of the cliff they saw a tangled mass of branches and splintered trunks.

So many shocking things had happened during the day that wonders were losing their sharpness, and they were soon, stoically, examining the cliff almost as coolly as though it were only some trivial geological object.

She had an abundant inner strength, as she recovered fast and appeared to be relaxed and charming within a few minutes. It did not take her much time to regain her composure. They noticed the extraordinary view over the forest, which they had traversed.

"Thanks John for helping me," mumbled Mitali with a charming smile. "You have done so much for me."

"I have done nothing special for you. Anybody would have done what I did, in such a situation."

"This is your benevolence and unconditional love," said Mitali. "You are a wonderful person."

He examined the bruise on her shoulder again. It was not deep, but some blood was still oozing out. He took out an ointment and aftershave lotion out of his pouch and softly cleaned the bruises with aftershave lotion and applied the ointment softly. She observed appreciatively that a cute, sweet, kind, attentive and loving stranger had become her nurse and helping her with tender care. Her first feeling was one of gratitude, blended with love. The glimmer of a charming smile began to show through her distress.

"Let us sit down for some time on that rock and enjoy the scenery," suggested Mitali looking into his eyes with a seductive smile.

"Be more comfortable Mitali," suggested John. They were both silent for many minutes. They sat there for some time. They were feeling now quite relaxed and joyful.

"I feel better now and I think we should move."

"Yes, good suggestion. Let us go," mumbled John standing up. "Be careful and walk slowly."

"You are so lovely and cute person. I wish I would have met you earlier," chuckled Mitali, after a brief pause. There was some hesitation, just a slight pause, during which she looked at John with her fond eyes.

He listened with the insatiable attention of a hungry soul. Every time she spoke, he looked into her face with affectionate eyes. "It feels fantastic to hear such lovely words from a gorgeous young lady like you."

He touched her hairs gently, putting back a stray curl that had fallen across her forehead and was hanging on her face. She got tired soon, after walking for some time. Both sat down comfortably and relaxed for a while. She reclined, putting her head in his lap and he feasted on her beauty.

He got up, holding her arm and suggested her to move. He tried to explore the area hoping to discover an adequately gentle slope, which Mitali might be able to descend safely and comfortably.

There were two ponds, one big and one small, in terraces descending the precipice. Both the ponds looked beautiful and enchanting. A range of hills, clothed with luxuriant vegetation and verdant grass, towered above them. There was a silence and the pellucid surface of water was unruffled by the abated breeze. There was no trace of human or animal life, except a few pigeons, swans and turtles, which were basking in the sun. Turtles plunged into the water, as they approached nearer. There was conglomeration of fishes in both ponds. They were leaping, frolicking, splashing, and scraping their sharp fins.

The clouds were still lingering behind the cliff, creating various golden patterns. The weather was, however, icy, as the cold breeze was still blowing. The exquisite hills appeared to slope sharply, almost precipitously, into the depth of the fresh-water ponds. They were flabbergasted to perceive such an attractive scenery. A hill rose two hundred feet above the water. The ponds were flanked by handsome trees, with flowering creepers clinging to their branches. Brilliant and colorful flowers, which were now in rich bloom, adorned these trees.

The water was running over a small rock and then splashing down from one pond to the other. From the second pond water was consistently cascading down in valley in misty torrents. The swans were frolicking on all the banks adding to the beauty of environment. A feeble and pleasant breeze touched their skin to create wonderful sensation.

"How do you feel now, Mitali? Is it still painful?" asked John with concern to highest pitch.

"No, not much, I can easily bear it now," cooed Mitali with a cute smile. "Thanks John, your care and touch has made lot of difference. The pain has considerably subsided. John, thank you for your care and comforting hugs. Your heavenly hugs made me forget everything else. I was in a dreamy state."

"It was not that type of hug, it was a simple safety hug," he chuckled laughing loudly.

"I do not think it was that simple," chuckled Mitali with a seductive smile. She was pleased and elated like a child. "Then tell me what 'that type of hug' is. I am eager to know the difference."

"She put her arms on his shoulders pulled him towards her, clasping him from back of his neck. He reciprocated with same passion and hugged her with a tight embrace. She closed her eyes, put her head on his shoulder and enjoyed the ecstasy for a long time."

"What you do and what are your hobbies?" asked Mitali, with her curiosity elevated to the highest pitch, while they were sitting down on the rock for relaxing and gasping for breath. "Where do you live and who is in your family, dear?"

"I am an industrialist and I inherited casting, forging and machining business from my father. My hobby is playing badminton, reading, travelling and cooking," mumbled john with a smile. I live at Poona with my mother and sister," said John. "What do you do, dear Mitali?"

"I am a TV artist and a model. I am fond of travelling, dancing, reading, listening to music and swimming."

"Very good. Are you married or have a boyfriend?"

"No, I am single. I have so many acquaintances, but no boyfriend, till a few hours before."

"Really? Thanks," John squeaked with a pleasant surprise. "What did you notice in my personality to elevate me to that pedestal of your heart?"

"I did not meet anyone like you earlier," chuckled Mitali with her usual charming smile. "You are a wonderful person, free from false ego. You are simple and unassuming personality."

She tried to grope around for more words, but she became emotional and became tacit and just glanced into his eyes. Adrenaline coursed through her veins quickening her pulse. She tried to explain, but could not find her voice.

Hearing her words, his hairs rose upon his head and a cold perspiration trickled down his cheeks. He was feeling euphoric to hear her words. He had a strange feeling, which, he had never experienced in his life earlier.

"I am impressed with your unbounded courage and perseverance. You, responsibly and admirably complete the task you undertake," muttered Mitali with a seductive smile.

"Thanks darling."

"You express your thoughts eloquently. Your hugs are even more eloquent," added Mitali with a charming smile, after a brief pause.

"So are my kisses." whispered John with a naughty smile, holding her tight. She responded with a hug and gently moved away. "Really? Let the time come to find out. Wait for intuitive nudge from within."

"It is very much there, my darling."

"Do not be so desperate. Let it come from both sides," she squeaked with a seductive smile.

"Okay, sweetie."

"I will like to pluck the plums from this tree," she insisted with child-like simplicity and tried to venture into safer ground and deftly tried to change the topic.

She tried to pluck them, but could not reach the point, in spite of her best efforts. He bent down to hold her legs and raised her above ground. She was thrilled to climb and pluck a few plums easily.

"Thank you dear for helping," she chirped delightfully like a child. "I like to pluck fruits from trees."

"Pleasure was all mine," he stuttered with wicked gleam dancing in his eyes.

They started walking again. She caught a sudden glimpse of John and realized that he was stepping with apparent ease over huge heaps of stones and fallen pieces of rock at the downward slope. Both of them were making their toilsome way down the slope. She hesitated and slowed down to walk more carefully. She had to struggle frantically and incessantly, rocking backward and forward on uneven terrain to maintain her equilibrium.

Noticing her hesitation, he came to her and held her hand in his hand. The sun was in its full splendor and it blazed with rays slanting down upon the hills, as she walked shuddering, wet with perspiration.

They continued walking cautiously and slowly with hand in hand. They noticed so many gorgeous wild flowers in the way. Both walked about the place, sat down on an elevated rock. They took rest and after some time, slowly started descending the slope. They slowly scaled down and stood mesmerized, for some time, looking at the serpentine river, meandering through jungle, down on the plains. Lush green jungle stretched out in front of them, in a wide sparkle of purest slanting sunlight.

"What a wonderful view on the plains below!" exclaimed Mitali with delight. "You made me extremely happy sweetie. I am really 'on top of the hill'."

"Yes honey," John cooed joyfully.

He slowed down considerably and descended slowly, giving support to Mitali, when he observed her hesitation to move with ease.

It did not take much time to walk to the point where they had parked the car. They were happy that they came together for a pleasant long drive and subsequent trekking. It was a wonderful experience of their lives.

Chapter-8

"Today we are going to another wonderful spot; the floating restaurant and we will have our breakfast and lunch there only. I hope you all had tea in your room.

"Yes," all murmured in unison.

"We will continue there, till 6 in the evening. I assure you, this is going to be a stunning experience for you all and you will always relish memory of this visit," Vikas assured with a jubilant smile. "Let us go and saunter along a few steps. Boat has arrived and is waiting for us on the sea shore."

"This restaurant is booked for us only. There will be no one else except us, the participants," explained Shams. "I did not want that there should be any distraction."

"Thank you, Shams," mumbled Vikas with a smile.

When they reached there, the boat had already arrived. All boarded the boat. It was a wonderful experience to sail on the boat. Cold sea breeze rejuvenated everybody.

"May I sit here?" asked Vinod, looking at Dr. Meena.

"Please, sit down," she said with a smile, setting her tresses hanging on her face and moving a side. "You might be sailing often and enjoying a lot on your own luxury boat."

"Yes, Dr. Meena," said Vinod. "As you know, I sailed up to this island by my own boat."

"It is a wonderful hobby," mumbled Dr. Meena joyfully. "I wish I could also get an opportunity to sail the long distances in a sea."

"Yes, Dr. Meena, sailing is my hobby. I like to spend plenty of time in the sea. I, once, cruised to Singapore by this boat. I participated in a few long distance races also. I like to spend most of my evenings on the boat," said Vinod. "I will like to share some moments with you on my boat, if you do not have any objection."

"I will be happy to have that experience," cooed Meena after some hesitation. She yielded to his entreaties and consented to go out with him. "I will love to have this wonderful experience with you," asserted Meena after a brief pause. "I never went for such an outing earlier, but I feel like going out with you."

"Let us get down, we have arrived at the venue," mumbled Vikas. They alighted stepping on a wooden platform connected to floating restaurant. The floating restaurant was erected on a small island and it appeared to be floating in the sea.

The view was enchanting with breath taking scenery. The sun was rising above the sea, and all the doves were ready for flight. The younger doves also imitated their elders to spread its wings for journey.

"Breakfast buffet is waiting for us. Being a doctor you very well know the importance of nutritious breakfast."

"Yes Vinod, I feel the aroma of something delicious," said Dr. Meena. "Breakfast is the most important meal of the day. Always make sure that you start your day with a nutritious and healthful breakfast. It will go a long way to provide your body and mind with adequate vigor and vitality," elaborated Dr. Meena. "Never skip it, as you are likely to become tired, when your brain and body run low on fuel. You require extra energy to joyfully start your day."

Dr. Meena turned towards Shams and Sofia and chirped with her usual smile, "You have made wonderful arrangement, Shams and Sofia; there are so many items to relish."

"We are happy, you liked it," said Sofia. "We have kept variety, taste and freshness in mind, while arranging it."

"Today, we have a combination of North and south Indian food," said Shams. "I am sure you will love it."

"Should I bring omelet for you?" asked Mitali with desperate eagerness, moving toward Reena.

"No, I will like to take idli and vada with Sāmbhar and mixed juice," said Reena. "Thank you very much, dear."

"I hope, everybody has enjoyed the breakfast," said Vikas. "Please be comfortable and sit relaxed. Have a few deep relaxing breaths and close your eyes. Try to recognize 5 different types of sounds you hear. Feel the silence between two sounds. Keep your whole body limp and relaxed," explained Vikas. "If you notice any tension in any part of your body, stretch that part, while inhaling and relax it, while exhaling. Take every tense part, one by one, and relax that part. Continue, as long as, you feel comfortable and your body is relaxed. Your senses will respond more efficiently, when your body is relaxed."

"I hope you all feel totally relaxed. Now open your eyes," said Vikas after a pause of a few minutes. "We will be here up to 6, in the evening, as I told you earlier. After that, we will move around by boat and spend some time in the vicinity around this exotic location. We are going to have a wonderful day today. How do you feel now and how did you like the place?"

"It is magnificent start of the day," said Reena delightfully. "It is pleasing experience. I am very happy."

"Relaxed and happy," responded Vinod with a smile. "I feel wonderful."

"It is beautiful place," cooed Dr. Meena. "It is an amazing experience to attend this workshop and interact with magnificent persons."

"It is an awesome feel to see water everywhere around this beautiful small island. It gives an appearance of floating," chimed in Mitali, joyfully. "It is a magnificent experience to spend a day here."

"Now sit still for a few minutes, focus in the moment, set intention of the day and visualize a marvelous day ahead."

"How do you feel now, Sofia?" queried Vikas, noticing the trace of despair on her face.

"I feel terrific, but sometimes guilt feelings of past and worries about future creep in."

"You are not alone to have such feelings. This, sometimes, happens with all of us," explained Vikas. "We should take an effective step, if such feelings persist and continuously bother us."

"What type of steps do you suggest?" asked Sofia.

"If we live in the present moment, focused in 'now', we will be happier and more successful in life. Past is already dead and over. Today is a new day and a fresh start," said Vikas. "Allow only positive thoughts to enter your mind and have positive mental attitude. With a positive mental attitude, our lamentation may well turn to elation. We will see that the gloom, which is a noticeable feature of the thought, will disappear. Live in this moment and enjoy your life. Take care of your body today; nurture, nourish and exercise it."

"I agree, Vikas. Most of time we are not living in the moment," Reena interjected. "Most of our energy is sapped by guilt and worries. But how can we overcome this destructive habit?"

"Solution lies in observing your mind and controlling thinking," expatiated Vikas. "Notice what is going on in your mind, in this moment. Always ask yourself, if you are present in the moment or thinking about past and future?"

"Mostly, I dwell in the present moment, but, sometimes, guilt feelings of past and worries about future creep in unnoticed," said Reena.

"This will not happen, if you are totally present and aware in the moment. If you just observe what is going on in your mind, you can easily monitor your thoughts. You will be present in the moment and you will be able to control the entry of undesirable thoughts," explained Vikas. "Then you can allow only those thoughts, which are related to the present moment."

"You can, actually live only in the present moment, not in past and future," Vikas elaborated further. "Yesterday is gone, tomorrow is yet to come and Life exists in this moment. This moment will also soon become the past. Today and now, in this moment, you have a wonderful opportunity to convert this moment into a beautiful memorable past. You can, very well, do this with focused awareness, unconditional love, and positive intention. Whatever you do, do it in this moment. Plan, forgive, take corrective action and analyze thoughts in this moment."

"I agree with you. We fritter away our maximum time and energy thinking about the past and worrying about the future," commented John. "What else should we do to remain in the present?"

"Analysis, awareness and asking questions are of tremendous importance," Vikas delineated. "Ask yourself: What is going on in my mind? Am I aware and in control of thoughts entering my mind? Am I present in the moment? What problems do I have now? Am I going to correct destination? Am I enjoying my journey? What is wrong with this moment?"

"Besides finding honest answers of these questions, repeat in your mind the affirmations; 'I am present here and now… My attention is also here and now in this moment… This exquisite day has been created by God… I will make best of this day by living with gusto in this moment and living in the day-tight compartment up to the bed time…' You should repeat these auto-suggestions till you subconscious takes over," said Vikas. "This moment is a wonderful moment. You are alive and in good health this moment."

"What we are today is continuation of my past. Our identity is based on what we did in the past and our present is defined by my past. How can we neglect our past?" enquired Shams. "Future is also useful in many ways."

"You may visit past and future, when you are required to do so, but we should not dwell there all the time. Make your dwelling place in this moment only," explained Vikas. "We must restrain ourselves, most of the time, from living in the past and worrying about future."

"When we are, all the time, thinking about past, lot of time is wasted in doing so. We feel guilty about various past events. As a result, we are not able to focus our attention to actually live effectively in the present moment," explained Vikas. "I, therefore, appeal you to make your dwelling place in this moment and remain most of time in this moment. You may, however, visit past and future, for a short time, when practical situations are to be dealt with."

"You mean to say that past and future is also useful," asked Reena.

"Yes, both are very useful," explained Vikas. "Past is useful for analyzing your past mistakes and feelings guilt and taking corrective action in the present moment to get rid of guilt feelings. You may improve your performance in the present moment, learning from past follies. You may also relish happy memories of past, time to time and boost your energy and get motivation. The problem arises when we make our dwelling place in the past and waste our energies, which we can, otherwise, use living our life fully in the present moment."

"Very well explained," said Sofia. "What about future?"

"Future is useful for planning, setting intention and visualization. It is essential to look ahead to plan the steps, we are going to take today," reiterated Vikas. "Live in now and visit, time to time, past and future when necessary. Life exists in this moment only. Be present, therefore, in this moment, most of the time."

"Does anybody want to ask any question, before I take up another topic after lunch?" asked Vikas. "After lunch, we will take up 'Slow Down to the Speed of Life' and making 'Constant Never Ending Improvements in all the fields'."

"I do not want to ask anything, but I want to share a real life story," Shams interposed.

"Okay, go ahead," Vikas prodded.

"A friend of mine was very studious and a man of erudition. He wanted to become an eloquent public speaker. He did not have, however, enough courage to go on stage because of stage fright. He was living in the future and was dreaming to become a speaker," said Shams. "I persuaded him to live in the present and prepare his speech thoroughly and avail the first opportunity to go on stage. I encouraged him to enroll in a public speaking course and avail every opportunity to speak in front of crowd. He, initially, hesitated and could not perform well, but soon, after some time, he spoke with confidence and he became a famous speaker."

"Very good," said Vikas. "Your motivation and his perseverance worked wonders."

"The story does not end here. Unfortunately, later, he had to face surgery of his tongue and part of his tongue had to be removed. He lived in the past and felt guilty of not starting speaking early in his life. I again persuaded him to live in the present and use his talent in writing. Writing had been his second best passion. He became successful writer."

"Spectacular example of a mighty comeback!" exclaimed Reena. Everybody clapped with applause and appreciation.

"Yes; he is still hopeful of becoming a good speaker again after another surgery and implant," Shams added. "There are so many examples of people who have metamorphosed their life by living in the present moment. We should concentrate our energies in this moment to get success and happiness in life."

"Wonderful example Shams, thanks," Vikas muttered with his usual smile. "I think we have discussed enough on this topic. We need a break. I do not think there is a better way to rejuvenate than have a wholesome lunch together. Come on, let us enjoy lunch break."

All congregated for lunch and had lunch in a joyful mood. Lunch was steamy, aromatic and delicious.

"Should I bring something for you, Meena?" asked Vinod, inching towards her with his plate.

"Thanks, Vinod, I have already taken enough in my plate," mumbled Meena with a lovely smile. "What have you learned today, Vinod?"

"Be present and enjoy now, in this moment, without postponing things for future," whispered Vinod in her ears with butter-soft voice. He appeared to be in a funny mood. "A kissed B yesterday or A will kiss B tomorrow, is not important. A is kissing B now, is important."

"Your replies are funny and crazy, are not they? You are so incorrigible that even an efficient Doctor like me, is helpless and is unable to cure you," said Dr. Meena laughing with suppressed voice.

It was a wonderful break. Everybody joked and enjoyed the break laughing hilariously. When they entered the place, Vikas was already sitting relaxed.

"Welcome back everybody… Let us start…"

"Good change. This time you are not going to start with meditation," chirped Reena with a smile.

"Please do not misunderstand. Meditation is a sine qua non for focused concentration and acquiring the receptive mode," said Vikas laughing with hilarity. "Close your eyes… sit relaxed… Take easy and deep breaths… Continue breathing… till you feel relaxed… Now, please raise one leg and trace imaginary alphabets with toe in space… keep relaxed… keeping your eyes closed. Then raise another leg and repeat the exercise again with other toe… Now relax and slow down… breath normally and easily with effortless ease."

Everybody followed his instructions.

"If you want to accomplish more, slow down to the speed of life," expatiated Vikas, initiating the discussion in a relaxed manner. "Whatever you do, do with slow pace. Slow down deliberately, when you notice yourself working with a frenzied pace."

"We have got so many things to do. If we slow down, we will be able to do less work. Which, in turn, will create more stress," Sofia muttered. "Sometimes, concentration is also less when we slow down."

"On the contrary, we accomplish more by slowing down. The concentration is also more in that case and there are fewer mistakes," Vikas shot back. "What is use of running with frenzied speed, when we are reaching nowhere? Most of our efforts are wasted without getting our passionate desires fulfilled."

"I agree. When there is more speed, we are full of stress and commit more mistakes. At the same time, we lose our peace of mind," interjected Mitali. "There is more need to slowdown in today's hectic life to live a more meaningful life."

"Yes, slow down to the speed of life and do everything with effortless ease, in a relaxed manner. You will notice what is happening around," Vikas uttered with his usual composure. "Enjoy the fragrance of flower and scenery en route to your office."

"There is another advantage of a slow paced life," Vikas reiterated and further explained. "When we are slow, we are more aware of what we are doing. We are able to focus our energy in what we are doing. We will automatically improve your performance. Just be aware to make constant never ending improvements in all the fields."

"I agree Vikas. With more focus on what we are doing, chances of committing mistakes will be considerably reduced," added Vinod after a brief pause. "You will make constant never ending improvements in all the fields. Do, therefore, less and slow down to achieve more, enjoy more and learn more."

"Which are the areas in which slowing down is more beneficial?" asked Sofia, her face lit up with curiosity and eagerness. "Which activities should we do more slowly?"

"We should slow down in all areas of life," said Vikas. "There is a very appropriate quotation by John De Paola: *'Slow down and everything you are chasing will come around and catch you.'* Slow down, therefore, to do more, to enjoy more and to accomplish more."

"Slowing down is helpful in every area of life, but we should be more slow and aware when we are travelling or driving," Vikas explained further. "We spend most of our time in driving on the roads. If we do not make the best of our journey, the trip is almost wasted. Enjoy, therefore, every moment of journey by slowing down, as journey is always more important than destination."

"Thanks Vikas," said Sofia.

"Driving slowly and enjoying every moment in the natural landscape is like a medication against anxiety and stress," interposed Dr. Meena.

"Thank you, Dr. Meena," Vikas muttered.

"Slowing down means; making time to appreciate your mornings by walking and driving slow, instead of rushing off to work in frenzy. You will enjoy the journey and you will know where you are going," explained Vikas. "Eddie Cantor has correctly expressed, when he said: '*Slow down and enjoy life. It's not only the scenery you miss by going too fast-you also miss the sense of where you are going and why*.' Appreciate your moments, slowing down and being present in the moment."

"To be precise, slow down or stop for a while to enjoy the ambience, hear chirping of birds and rustle of leaves in the forest, view the enchanting scenery and take wonderful pictures," said Vikas. "Appreciate your environment by slowing down and relishing every moment. By slowing down, you will also have a plentiful time at your disposal to peacefully contemplate your life as a whole... Any comments Dr. Meena?"

"You have cogently explained to us," said Dr. Meena. "The ability to act slowly is immensely helpful. The frantic pace of modern life, as you have already explained, takes a serious toll on your bliss, serenity and health. When you slow down, you get plentiful time for setting priorities for doing things in order of importance and achieving quality results. You will be free from stress, which is source of various ailments."

"Thanks, Dr. Meena," said Vikas. "By slowing down your speed, and focusing on the present moment, you can achieve significant productivity and creativity. At the same time, you will maintain a calmer state of mind, free from stress."

"As I mentioned earlier, another important area is eating," Vikas reiterated. "Do not just gobble down your food, but eat slowly to reverse the frenzied lifestyle. Take smaller bites, and chew each bite slower and longer. You will eat less, enjoy your meal longer and digest it more easily by slowing down your eating."

"I agree with you Vikas. Slow eating is beneficial for weight loss and improved health also," Dr. Meena explained further, "as we consume fewer calories."

"Why?" asked Vinod. "Can you explain in detail?"

"The reason is that it takes about 20 minutes for our brains to register that we are full," explained Dr. Meena. "If you eat slower, you will enjoy every bite and eat less quantity of food. You will chew your food better, savoring every nibble, which leads to better digestion."

"You have clearly explained to us, Dr. Meena," said Vinod appreciatingly. "Thank you very much."

"Thanks Dr. Meena," said Vikas. "We should all take precautions to deliberately eat slower."

"I want to add here one more point. Serve yourself only small quantity of food, to begin with," said Vikas. "Every time you put morsel in your mouth, put your fork down. After you have chewed your food well, only then put another morsel in your mouth."

"Let me add a few more points here, Vikas," interposed Dr. Meena. "Chew your food, as much as you can and pay attention to texture, taste and substance. The more you chew your food, the more you will feel full and be able to swallow the same properly. Drink water in between bites. Water helps us feel full, helps in the digestion process and works as a detoxifying agent. Talking through a meal, but not while chewing, can make you halt and slow down your eating habits."

"Thanks, Dr. Meena, for your valuable contribution," said Vikas. "Your suggestions are very useful for us."

"There is one more area, in which slowing down helps a lot," said Vinod, with a naughty smile.

"What is that?"

"In love making," added Vinod, joyfully with a naughty wide grin.

"Yes Vinod, I agree," said Vikas with a smile, "but I do not think, there is a need to go in detail. You are all intelligent and grownup."

"You are correct, Vikas. And also there is no need to share our experiences," squeaked Vinod laughing. Everybody laughed with hilarity.

"What are you planning to do in the evening," whispered Vinod in the ears of Dr. Meena. "I want to spend a few beautiful moments with you."

"Cannot you wait for the evening? Do not you see we are in the workshop? Be here now in this moment," asserted Meena softly, with feeble smile. "Tell me why you are so desperate?"

"I want to practice magnificent principles taught in this workshop," whispered Vinod with naughty smile. "I want to make slow love."

"Shut up, Vinod. I mistook you a good person," blurted out Meena, with a false annoyance but a butter-soft voice. "Cannot you be serious?"

"No private discussions, please. If you must discuss something, you must involve me also."

"*I cannot involve you my dear Vikas in this lovely conversation with my sweetheart,*" Vinod thought and wanted to say. He simply nodded with a smile, but said nothing. He noticed that Meena was constantly looking at him with inquisitive eyes.

"I, very well, know what you are thinking naughty boy," Whispered Meena with a smile, trying to read his enigmatic smile. "You require a few more such workshops to cleanse your thoughts."

"Now we will have hot tea, coffee and snacks, said Vikas with a smile. "Then you can have a walk and enjoy the ambience. After sometime, we will discuss de-cluttering and constant never ending improvements in all fields."

Everybody returned relaxed and joyful.

"Stand up, everybody," Vikas instructed. "First let us clap vigorously and then dance to generate some energy and rejuvenate." Everybody followed his instructions.

"We have a tendency to pile up the things, which we do not require. We have plenty of clothes, which we will never wear," Vikas elucidated. "For living peaceful and happy life, we should be free from clutter."

"What do you think, is the reason for unnecessary clutter?" asked Vikas. "Why do we pile up things which we do not require?"

"In most of the cases, I think, the reason for clutter to arise is that we love things more than we love people," said Mitali. "Leslie Bibb has correctly said: *'My friends tease me because I don't like clutter. I'm not someone who gets attached to things.'* We should always remember that people are more important than things."

"Thanks Mitali for your observations," said Vikas. "When you wake up in the morning, you might have noticed that de-cluttered house gives us peace, joy, contentment and satisfaction. Similarly, a de-cluttered and ordered workspace also brings an enormous harmony and order. Simon Cowell said: *'I hate belongings. I hate clutter. It really bothers me because I can't think properly. If you've got distractions in front of you, your mind goes nuts.'* We must, therefore, de-clutter our place, mind and life at the earliest opportunity."

"What is the most effective way to de-clutter?" asked John, inquisitively. "Things go on increasing, day-by-day, as life progresses."

"You are correct Mr. John. De-cluttering is easy and simple, if we keep certain things in our mind. Just be aware and find out the things, you, no more, require," said Vikas. "It does not take much time, but benefits are long-lasting and abundant. Make it a regular habit to do de-cluttering 10 minutes in one room daily."

"Can you be a bit more specific?" asked Vinod.

"There may be a few items or dresses in your room, which you have not used for 6 months. There may also be items, which you will never use in future," said Vikas. "You must dispose of these items at the earliest. Brian Greene said: *'I can't stand clutter. I can't stand piles of stuff. And whenever I see it, I basically just throw the stuff away.'* We must de-clutter what we do not require."

"I think the best thing is not to allow thing to pile up," interjected Sofia. "We have tendency to impulsively purchase the things. One way to have a more clutter-free home is to pause and ponder before purchasing anything.

We, sometimes, purchase duplicate items, because we generally forget that we already had the same."

"Yes Sofia, you are correct. If we are just aware, we will not allow the clutter to pile up. We must think twice before we purchase anything," said Vikas. "You may have books and magazines galore, which you are not going to read. There is a need to de-clutter every corner of your house. You may de-clutter your old receipts or your old magazines."

"How to actually do it?" asked Mitali. "Suggest some practical ways."

"Good question. To start with, get a few bags or boxes. Make four piles, one the stuff you want to keep. Pile number two is worthless, broken or terribly outdated, which you will never need in your life. Pile number three is the stuff you don't want or need, but is still worth something. Pile number four is for items you can sell," explained Vikas. "Do it for 15 minutes daily, till everything is in order. You will feel light, relaxed and joyful."

"Or you can put the things you want to keep, in one of the boxes and what you want to sell or give in charity, in the other box," said Vikas. "Donate the items which are useful for others. De-cluttering will allow you experience the joy of giving and others the joy of receiving. Remaining items, which you want to keep, may be set or stored at a proper place."

"Sometimes, unfinished domestic work also creates unnecessary clutter," Sofia explained. "We should promptly do dishes and wash cloth to clear the space and put everything in order at proper place."

"Marvelous suggestion. Take 5 minutes to do the dishes, take 5 minutes to fold the laundry and put at proper place," expatiated Vikas. "Do not let these things pile up here and there. Store everything in a systematic manner. Stack everything properly and let there be a place for everything."

"You should always keep in mind that de-cluttering should be done at the earliest opportunity," Vikas added after a brief pause.

"Why?" asked Reena.

"Delay causes more problems," retorted Vikas. "Johnathan Hunter said: *'You only take the garbage out once - because if you bring it back inside, the next time you have to take it out, it's just that much harder, heavier, and stinks even more! Relationships are the same.'* De-clutter at the earliest opportunity."

"You are correct; the earlier action you take to de-clutter, the better," said John.

"Another point to keep in mind is to start doing de-cluttering systematically. Select a corner or area that needs the maximum attention for de-cluttering," said Vikas. "This area may be the room that is in the worst shape, one that will give you the enhanced sense of accomplishment. Begin sorting through things in that area and work your way around the room, until you have gone through the room with a fine tooth comb."

"I have found that using boxes with labels, is a better way to store magazines, toys and other miscellaneous things that, otherwise, lie scattered here and there," said Dr. Meena.

"Yes, Dr. Meena. Donate items that you no longer require. Throw away garbage or items that others wouldn't benefit from," said Vikas. "Once all things that do not belong to this room are removed, you will have a better idea of how to organize the room."

"Sometimes, not only things, but ideas also bother us," said Reena with a smile. "We are flooded with undesirable ideas."

"You are correct, Reena. We must de-clutter our ideas, thinking and life as well," said Vinod. "Tell me, Mr. Vikas, how we can effectively do it?"

"Monitor your thoughts and do not let the negative ideas enter your mind without your permission. Limit the number of TV shows and films you watch, by deciding in advance, which TV programs are useful. Limit the use of internet and chatting. De-clutter your e-mail box by promptly reading, sending appropriate replies and deleting," said Vikas. "Take full responsibility of what you feel and think. You are master of your destiny. Take charge of your life."

"You can control ideas, but what about people who pester a lot and make gratuitous remarks?" asked Mitali smiling. "There are so many persons who poke their nose all the time, whether we like it or not. How can I overcome such problems?"

"Good point, Mitali. This is a genuine problem, especially for gorgeous young ladies like you," said Vikas laughing. "It is your life; you should know and decide what type of relationship you should maintain and with whom. You should also know how to say 'no' when you want to say 'no'. You should tell the nosey parkers clearly, where their nose ends and your work begins."

"Thanks," said Mitali. "Very good suggestion, indeed."

"There is a need to de-clutter your relationship also. You should clearly know what you require from a relationship. When you know what you want and need from relationships, a door opens to you," Vikas suggested. "Ask yourself these questions: *What do I want? What am I getting? Is there a gap between what I want and what I am getting?*"

"I think, we have continued our discussion for a long time. You all might be feeling bored now. We need a well-deserved break. Do not we?" said Vikas with a smile. "Stand up in a queue, one behind the other, faces in my direction. Massage shoulders of person in front of you with both the hands."

"Who will massage my shoulder?" asked Mitali, who was standing in the end, laughing. All followed his instructions.

"Have patience, Mitali… Continue for 2 minutes," said Vikas laughing. "Now, turn back, everybody… Massage shoulders of person in front of you, as you did earlier."

"Is it now okay, Mitali?" asked Vikas laughing.

"Yes, Vikas," said Mitali with her usual smile.

"We are going to meet tomorrow in the evening also, 2 Hrs. after workshop, before dinner. You all get ready for dinner, but reach directly to central hall. We will practice giving presentation. Everybody will be given 2 minutes time to give presentation. You may take help of power point files or you may bring your own audio-visual files. One minute time will be given to everybody for question answer session. After every presentation, audience will put questions to the presenter and presenter will try to satisfy the audience. The audience will also give feedback about the presentation, just after it is done."

"What is the topic of presentation," asked Sofia inquisitively. "We should be given the topic, so that we can prepare in advance."

"I give you very simple topic," said Vikas. "Topic is 'Success'. You may think about it, rehearse it, prepare it and practice it."

"It is not easy to talk briefly about a vast topic," said Reena laughing.

~~~

"Who will like to speak first?" asked Vikas.

"Okay, I will speak first," said Shams with alacrity and reached to the dais.

"Good morning ladies and gentlemen. My name is Shams and I work here in this resort. Today's topic of discussion is, 'Success'. Success is a vast subject like Happiness. Success has different meaning for different persons. For me, success means achievement of one's coveted desires. Setting lofty goal and accomplishing it gives me maximum satisfaction," said Shams, starting the presentation. "Our minor goals should be in conformity with the vision and missions in life, otherwise our energy is wasted and result remains elusive."

He paused for a moment and took deep breath. He took special care to use pleasant voice. He spoke with confidence, looking in the eyes of audience, one by one.

"I regularly set my daily and weekly goals and follow them sincerely. Setting priority is also important while setting our goals. We do not have much time, therefore, we should use it properly," added Shams after a brief pause.

"Any question from audience?" asked Vikas.

"Do not you think that too much discipline and adherence to goals reduces creativity?" asked Sofia.

"I do not think so, replied Shams. "On the other hand, time will be utilized in a better manner and more work will be performed by sticking to schedule. Without it, we will be moving like a rudderless boat."

"Anybody wants to give feedback?"

"Pace and projection was good. He spoke with confidence, but sometimes movements were stiff and looked like that of robot. Eye contact and movement was quite good. It was a good speech," said Sofia.

"Now it is your turn, Mr. John," said Vikas with a smile.

"Ladies and gentlemen, my name is john and I am a business man," said John. "Once a disciple perfumed penance for 12 years. God was pleased and He granted him his wish. Accordingly, he was able to walk on water. When he apprised to his master that he can walk on water after penance for 12 years, the master admonished him for waste of time. He said, 'You have wasted 12 years in vain. You could have easily crossed the river spending only a penny.' The disciple realized his mistake," John narrated the story to grab the attention of the audience. "Mr. Shams has correctly told us importance of setting priority and doing things in order of importance."

"Working incessantly and sincerely for achieving goals gives us immense satisfaction. If we are able to sincerely work for our goals, we feel that we are successful, even if we do not get immediate results."

"Any question from anybody?"

Nobody buzzed to ask question, but Shams nodded to say something.

"He started the presentation with a story. It is a suitable way to create the interest and grab the attention of the audience. He put forward his points precisely and eloquently. He spoke with power and professionalism. It was an amazing speech," said Shams.

"I liked his natural style, free from any stress," said Sofia. "His movements and gestures were confident. I think, he should elaborate his points further and there is need for more coherence."

"Now, it is your turn, Mr. Vinod," said Vikas.

"Good morning friends. For me, success and happiness are synonymous. I want to be happy, so long as I am alive. If I am happy, I feel that I am successful, even if I do not get tangible results," asserted Vinod with confidence. "I have an excessive appetite for adventure. Adventure gives me immense joy and joy, in turn, gives me feeling of success. I do not equate success with lofty results."

"If I am happy during making sincere efforts to get what I want, that is enough for me. I am contented, even if I do not get the results. Sincere efforts and sacrifices are important for achieving success. Working smart is more important than working hard," continued Vinod. "You will get more results with fewer efforts, though I believe that getting success is not easy. It requires us to come out of our comfort zone to get to the pinnacle. Success requires dedication and sacrifice. You might have heard the name of Tennis player Simona Halep. She had gone the extra mile to succeed and get to the zenith of her game. She had to undergo breast reduction surgery to improve her performance. Her sacrifice to take risk and undergo the surgery has played an important role to help her reach the pinnacle."

"Be passionate about your chief mission. First of all locate something you love and you will find the way to get to your zenith. Decide what actions you contemplate and how you are going to monitor your progress. Another reason most will not get to the summit is that they refuse to confront obstacles and challenges. You can always get better and getting better will help you climb higher peaks. Your progress may be slow but steady. Do not stop climbing, persist and persevere. By following these tips in your life, I am sure, you will succeed in your mission of life and you will reach the top of the ladder of success."

Nobody asked any question, but Reena offered to give her feedback. She said, "It was a wonderful speech and he eloquently put forth his points of view. He has covered so many points in a short time. Movements were smooth and eye contact was good. He narrated an interesting story to successfully create an interest in his presentation."

"Mitali, it is your turn now," said Vikas.

"Good morning friends. I am Mitali. Like previous speakers, I also agree that setting goals is very important to achieve success in life. First brain storm to decide what you are passionate about. Fix your target and start working with positive mind," said Mitali. "You should have a mechanism to monitor the goals. Once you set the goals and fix your target, adhere to them and do not change them frequently," added Mitali after a brief pause. "As Vinod has said, working smart is more important than working hard for reaching top."

"Never blame your luck. God is always a good God with a very big battalion. He is always there to extend all possible help. We should be grateful to Him for all His blessings and for rewarding our efforts to succeed," added Mitali. "The more sincere efforts we make, the more we succeed and more self-confidence we gain. With more self-confidence we get more success."

She paused for a few moments and then continued with confidence, "Do your self-analysis and introspection to succeed in life. Determine your passions. Determination, optimism and positive thinking are the hallmarks of success. Always think positive and be optimist, whatever the circumstances."

She paused for some time to ponder and take a deep relaxing breath and then continued again with a relaxed mind, "Dreams are precursors of success. Keep your thinking lofty. Hope for the best, but be prepared for the worst. Do not be disheartened by temporary setbacks. These are the challenges to make you stronger to face the bigger challenges of life."

"Any questions or feed backs from anybody?" asked Vikas.

"She started in a natural and relaxed manner and expressed her points cogently. Her eye contact was good and she looked briefly in eyes of everybody. She spoke with cool confidence. It was a wonderful speech," said Vinod.

"Now, Sofia will express her views," said Vikas.

"Without going into etymology of the word 'success', I consider myself successful, if I have lived well, smiled and laughed often, and loved much. To me, success means, gaining respect of intelligent men and the love of children," started Sofia with conviction. "I consider the person successful, if he sets a goal and achieves it without hurting others. A successful man always leaves the world better than he found it."

Sofia took a brief pause and started speaking again, "He appreciates beauty of nature and lives a simple life. He looks best in others and manifests his best. He readily comes out of his comfort zone to help others. He is a go-giver and gives for the joy of giving. He knows that real happiness is achieved by making others happy. Success and happiness are inter connected."

"Thanks. Any questions or comments, Shams?" asked Vikas.

"The presentation is too short. She should have included a few more points in her speech. She emphasized happiness more than success. The style, body language and eye contact was very good. She spoke confidently," Shams commented.

"Thanks for your comments and feedback, Mr. Shams," said Sofia. "I do not agree with you on one point. You will agree with me that there is a strong connection between success and happiness and success very much depends on happiness. If you are happy about something, you will be more attracted to it. What you are attracted to, expands. You get what you are attracted to. When we achieve our desired passions, we are successful."

"Very well explained, Sofia." said Vikas. "Reena, it is now your turn to speak."

"Good morning friends. I am Reena. I am a model and an actress. To me, success means, taking positive action with faith, hope and gratitude. We have to explore choices and options and take an effective action to get them," said Reena. "Once a reporter was asked by his editor to go and interview a certain man. The youngster asked: 'Where can I find him?' Smiling, the Editor replied: 'Wherever he is. Do not waste your time here. Go and find out.'"

"We must create our own opportunities; otherwise, we will become children of circumstance," continued Reena. "Diffidence is a species of cowardice. It causes a man's courage to ooze out at his toes faster than it comes into his heart."

"Successful persons deal with the situation, as it is. They will say: 'I have a choice'... 'Here are our options'... or 'Let's imagine all the possibilities.' They will never say: 'It's not fair.' They, very well, know that claiming and exercising the power to choose is the first step towards achieving their goals and getting success in life."

"Successful people don't wallow in the past, and they rarely regret a decision or action. They accept it as a learning experience, which gets them one step closer to their goal. They help others succeed. We should prepare ourselves against unpleasant happenings by taking stock of our mental and physical assets at the very outset of our journey."

"Successful people are passionate about innovation, doing something new or finding a better way of doing something. To succeed, we should learn from everybody and from every source. Avoid sycophancy and impress by your work. You can't make everyone happy, but you can always give your best and manifest your best. Good health is also important for success. Maintain, therefore, good health."

"Comprehensive speech, indeed. She has efficiently covered so many points in her speech. She seems to have thoroughly prepared her speech," said Vinod. "She has spoken with courage, conviction and confidence."

"Now, Dr. Meena will express her opinion on the topic under discussion. Dr. Meena, it is your chance to speak," said Vikas, gesticulating at her with a smile.

"Good morning friends. My name is Meena and I am a successful doctor. I remember a very good quotation by Albert Einstein: *"If A is success in life, then A equals x plus y plus z. Work is x; y is play; and z is keeping your mouth shut."*

"I do not measure success with achievement. I believe that, if you have sincerely tried your best, you are successful. Work smart, not hard. Love your work and do your best playfully. Do not boast your achievement. Be laconic and speak concisely, effectively, forcefully and boldly."

She further added, "Why some people achieve success in life and others do not and why only 5% of the people really achieve success in life? If you do the same things as those around you, you have only 5% chances to achieve the success in a life. Here, innovation plays an important role, as my predecessor has emphasized."

"The first and the most important step to be successful in life is to find your own dream. Find out what you are passionate about. Sit down quietly and try to listen to yourself and your heart. Ask yourself, 'What do I want out of my life?' Take a sheet of paper and write down minimum 10 big dreams, then 40 important dreams, and finally 50 small dreams. When you find your dreams, decide the appropriate action plan to fulfill your dreams," said Dr. Meena.

She took brief pause then started to speak further, "Now you have to start taking action. Once action started, you are already on your way to success. Here are some tips for success to share with you; Dress up well and to the occasion and let your dress reflect your personality. Setting goals is not enough; you have to set deadlines and act to finish your work in time. Respect the time and utilize it properly. Completion of work in time will keep you free from stress. Have a mechanism to monitor your success and scrupulously monitor your progress."

"Will you like to give your feedback, Vinod?"

"She had, very confidently, started speaking with an appropriate quotation. She took very good points and elaborated in detail. She adroitly made her points clear. She spoke confidently like an expert speaker," said Vinod.

"Vikas, please give your general assessment and suggestions," said John.

"There are three parts of a speech; the beginning, the middle and the end. End is equally important; therefore we should never neglect it. The beginning should be interesting enough to grab attention of the audience. I have observed that nobody did recapitulation in the end. It is very important. We should wind up the presentation with memorable grand finale," Vikas explained. "Another important point is to keep in mind that people remember only 3 important points. We should decide, while preparing our speech, what these important 3 points are. Our speech should revolve around those three points."

I have observed that Mr. John and Reena had started their speeches with a story and Dr. Meena had started her speech with a quotation. These are amazing attention grabbers and create interest among the audience. Zestful remarks, jokes, quotations and stories create tremendous interest.

Chapter-9

Dr. Meena had woken up quite late this morning, revitalized and joyful. The morning was still cool and pleasant. Waking up late has not been too alien a concept to her. When she got up today, rays of light were darting through the crevices of the windows. The rising sun proclaimed the advent of another lovely day, full of many promises. The antique clock asseverated the advent of the wonderful day with seven distinct strokes. She sauntered ahead to open window and peep out. Her glance rested on bushes replete with beautiful, brilliant and colorful flowers. As she opened the window, the cold breeze mingled with fragrance of flowers entered the room to brush her face. It rejuvenated her spirits further.

This workshop was a magnificent experience of her life. She relished every moment of her stay here on this wonderful resort. She mused, *"I have wisely decided to come here. I relished every moment of stay here. I will never forget exquisite moments spent here."*

She was a famous doctor and her aim was to serve the people and put smile on the faces of maximum persons. She always believed that real happiness is achieved by making others happy. She had created a fund to spend in charity and provide medicine to the needy person who could not afford to purchase medicines and medical services. She came out of her comfort zone to inspire rich people and her colleagues to contribute in her noble venture.

She also realized that positive mental attitude and self-growth is as important as medicines and medical care. There is a close relationship between physical fitness and inner bliss. She thought that what she was learning and going to learn here was going to be of immense benefit in her profession and daily life.

The days flowed on delightfully. They were diversified and full of vitality and effervescence. Each day brought with it, something innovative, exotic, uplifting and inspirational. As usual, today also, she was feeling joyful, ebullient and hilarious. The fatigue of the evening before seemed to have vanished in the expectation of what was to happen today. She visualized in minute detail a wonderful day ahead. It became her usual practice after she came here. She whistled gaily while washing and getting fresh. She noticed magnificent change in her outlook, since she came to this resort to attend the workshop.

She was tacit by nature. She never expected that she would ever develop close friendship with someone. She was experiencing some peculiar change in her feelings shortly. She had a strange and a wonderful feeling, whenever she was with Vinod. Bond of intimacy was getting stronger day-by-day. As a result of her proximity with Vinod, her personality was metamorphosed beyond recognition. She was all the time thinking about him.

Today she was in a joyous spirit, as she was going for an outing with Vinod. She had accepted his proposal to spend a few hours with him on his boat. It was her first dating.

She appeared a rare blending of elegant face, shapely figure and marvelous complexion. She looked charming in light green dress, putting on pinkish red lipstick. Her elegant figure, consisting of its youthful roundness, agile flexibility, a dignified grace reminded a duck ready to pedal along gracefully in a lake. She looked charming and a marvelous model for a sculptor. Her blossoming face, juicy, red vivacious lips, with shining forehead, looked attractive. Her brilliant face vividly contrasted by the hanging black tresses.

She had heard about dating from her friends and had a desire to go for it to experience it first hand, but she could not dare due to some inhibitions. She also heard that people going for dating do all short of funny activities. She recalled:

Her friend, Neelam once told her, "I am going for dating today with my boyfriend."

"What is dating?" asked Meena, "and what exactly you do there."

"It is really a funny and strange query. Really, do not you know anything about of dating? Are you living in some strange world?" asked Neelam with naughty smile. "It is outing with a friend on stipulated date and time. It is up to you what you do there. You may go to any extreme to enjoy and have fun. You can also just go out, move around, have a hearty talk and come back, my sweet shy girl."

She was happy that she gathered courage to decide for going for dating this time with Vinod. She had dressed to the occasion, imagining his choice. She was happy when Vinod appreciated her earlier for her choices. She kept his choice and taste in mind, while deciding to choose her dress. She wanted to hear him say, *"Hi sweetie, you are looking gorgeous in this dress."*

Vinod was eagerly waiting for her when she reached. Dr. Meena looked so charming, he could not remove his glances for some time from her.

"How do I look?" asked Dr Meena blushing, noticing his constant gaze.

"You look ravishing. Who will not like such a lovely choice of dress? It is fabulous and couldn't be more stunning and perfect," chuckled Vinod laughing, looking at her shapely torso. She was a slim, fair and pretty woman. She had a rare charm and brilliance than is generally noticed. Her charm was immaculate, natural and unintentional and it abundantly appealed to senses and intellect.

"You look sexy and irresistible. You have lot of appeal." Vinod wanted to say, but he simply looked at her with his loving eyes and imbibed her charm. She felt strange rush of blood in her veins, when her eyes met his penetrating eyes. She could not bear his constant and intent gaze and lowered her glances blushing profusely. He could lucidly read her eloquent blushes, but she regained her composure said nothing.

"You look so cute and gorgeous. Today I realized that you look more appealing, when you blush," Vinod jested. "Your blushes are even more eloquent than your words. God has given you so many assets. You are a magnificent soul in a wonderful body," Vinod murmured looking at her with appreciation, after a brief pause.

She kept quiet and strived hard to control her blushing. She groped around to find suitable words to reply.

"Just relax honey. There is no need to reply in words. Blushing is an interesting and an effective substitute," cooed Vinod, raising her chin and looking deep into her eyes.

"Thank you Vinod for accolades," she mumbled, regaining her composure, with a charming smile. She just put her hand tentatively on his. Their hands clasped softly and silently.

"Are you nervous of sailing?" he asked softly, continuing to clasp her hand with his hand.

"Not at all," she dismissed mumbling softly, with a mild smile.

"You seem discomforted by your surroundings," said Vinod, looking into her eyes. "I hope you have trust in me?"

"Any doubt?" chimed in Meena with an enigmatic smile. "Otherwise, I would not have boarded the boat of a person, who would have taken me deep in sea, wherever he wanted to take me."

"No... to take you only where you want to go, Dr Meena," he corrected with a loud laugh. "Please trust, you are safest in my hand. Be relaxed and comfortable. This boat has all the facilities including a comfortable bed. I do not want to deprive you of your rest."

"I like your kind gesture and caring attitude. I feel joyful in your company," Meena mumbled with intent to change the topic.

"Thanks Meena for coming. You made my day wonderful," said Vinod with smile. "I was eager to spend some time with you."

"What is so special in me?"

"You have so many assets, including an enchanting smile. What a specimen of smile!" he chuckled. "Exquisite... ravishing... gorgeous... stunning. Where did you get hold of these charming assets?"

"Thanks Vinod for compliments. I am also glad," said Meena with a charming glow on her countenance. "I am eager to know more about you. You might be facing so many challenges in day-to-day life. Your job and your hobby of sailing, both are full of enormous adventure, are not they?"

"Yes, I love adventurous life. Adventure is in my blood."

"I am curious to know about you and your life," Meena chirped with her usual tempting smile. She was, by now, feeling more comfortable and less restrained to articulate with confidence. "I want to vicariously enjoy what you do."

"I inherited this beautiful luxury boat from my father. He was in shipping business and his hobby was also sailing and remaining in water most of the time. I used to go in the sea with him often," Vinod delineated with a smile, looking at her with fond eyes. "When I joined the sea customs, later, this hobby proved to be of enormous help to me in my profession also. My sailing experience helped me successfully chase the smugglers and book wonderful seizures of gold and drugs."

"I have noticed that you have a real adventurous spirit and you are fond of effervescent life."

"Yes dear; you are correct. I like sea because it is personification of enormous energy. It is always bubbling with enthusiasm and there is lot of action," said Vinod looking at her face, which was lit up with curiosity. She listened to him intently and interestedly, her glances constantly fixed on his face.

"What is other reason you love it?" asked Meena with a smile. "I am curious to know more."

"I love its vigor and energy in form of the breeze and the wind."

"Okay. You have to face storms and strong winds. Are not they dangerous? Why should you expose yourself to danger?" asked Meena with concern.

"There is no adventure without danger and risk. There is no life without adventure. You have to come out of your comfort zone to live a real life."

"You might have noticed formation of waves and storms," Meena prodded, encouraging him to speak more.

"Yes, I saw the formation and they are dangerous. Waves are caused by wind, which ruffles the surface of the sea into ripples. Acting with consistent enhanced influence on the surface thus raised, wind blows them up into waves, and finally into mighty billows," delineated Vinod.

"You might be finding it difficult to fight with huge waves, billows and storms when the wind is uncompromising."

"Yes, sometimes it becomes very risky. There is more adventure when more risk is involved," explained Vinod smiling. "I noticed a strange phenomenon in the sea."

"What?" she asked curiously.

"Sometimes winds are so infuriated that they do not allow the waves to move up their heads above the surface. Whenever waves try to raise their head, they are calmed down and disseminated in foam."

"It is a very interesting phenomenon, indeed. I have never noticed or heard such an occurrence. I think it is energy and adventure, which attract you," uttered Meena. "Is it the only aspect of personality of ocean, which you are attracted to?"

"My attraction is not restricted to that aspect only. You might also be aware of only one aspect of personality of oceans, Meena. I am also attracted to depth, tranquility and serenity of oceans," said Vinod looking deep into her eyes. He took her face between his hands, and bending over her, looked long and steadfastly into her eyes. "I am also attracted to unruffled serenity of the oceans. I have found that the depths of the ocean always remain unperturbed, serene and calm. Oceanic storms do not agitate the bottoms and the lowest points of the deep oceans. When the storm is pounding the surface of the sea into a state of violent agitation, the undersides of the depths are in the state of unspoiled tranquility, like your deep eyes."

"Again started. Are you all the time in a romantic mood, Vinod?" Meena chuckled with a charming smile.

"Not always, but only when I look deep into your eyes," squeaked Vinod. "Do not you like it?"

"I like it to some extent, but too much of everything is awful," said Meena laughing. "I also like your fantastic sense of humor."

"It is always advisable to look at the sunny side of life. Attitude makes a lot of difference to live a happy life. Touch of humor is necessary to the salvation of the tacit and serious lady like you. The mere cultivation of laughter and sense of humor awakens you to a feeling of the joy of living. They would eventually lead to perpetual inner bliss. Men with a sense of humor are the ones who stir the world with new desires and make life worth living. I, therefore, entreaty you to laugh, enjoy and live! To see the funny side of one's own achievement is wonderful."

"That is a magnificent philosophy. But it is also advisable to be a well behaved, controlled and responsible person."

"Look at me, sweetie, and see how responsible I am," he muttered, putting his hands softly on her shoulders and pressing softly. Before she could recover her composure, he hugged her with tight embrace. She realized that a strange tingling sensation and a delightful dreaminess were stealing over her. It took her time to respond with a tighter hug. "But, my dear Meena, you do not appear to be controlled. Your heart is hammering wildly."

She groped in vain for suitable words to respond, but she just blushed furiously and said nothing. She, however, managed charming smile in return.

"Are you happy?" asked Vinod with desperate eagerness and yet tender care.

"Yes, to be frank," she chuckled with a delightful smile. "I like you. You are wonderful person."

"In that case, you will not object me kissing you," said Vinod. "May I kiss you honey?"

She was stunned, but soon recovered her equanimity and looked enquiringly into his eyes, conjecturing whether he had really articulated those words or had she fancied them in her imagination.

"Be patient and do not always sail at frenzied speed Vinod," cooed Meena with enigmatic smile. "Slow down to the speed of life and enjoy all sceneries in the way. Be patient and wait for the appropriate time, darling. Wait for it and you will realize that it was worth a wait. In nature everything happens with slow pace. Fishes just swim and birds just fly with natural speed."

"Are you comfortable or should I reduce the speed of boat?"

"It is comfortable. You very well know that I am not talking about speed of the boat."

"How do you like sailing here with me in a deep sea?" he tried to change the topic to assuage her feelings.

"Wonderful."

"I suggest you to go back and look through the window of the boat," advised Vinod. "You will have an exquisite experience and enjoy magnificent view."

He had correctly advised her. It was a wonderful view from behind. The hosts of stars that studded the sky overhead, looked amazing, though they did not shed any appreciable light on the waters of the sea, on which the boat was moving fast. Full moon was in the sky and silvery moon light was falling on the wake of the boat. That beautiful and mysterious phosphorescence of moon illumined the froth which was gleaming brilliantly. The glowing trail of the wake of boat appeared to follow the boat like a serpent of lambent fire.

The sea, stretched out in a wide sparkle of purest blue and it shimmered with millions of tiny silvery ripples. She wondered whether it was a dream or a reality. There is time in one's existence when actualities appear to be delicate shadows of a dream and dreams blossom with astonishing brilliance of reality.

She abruptly came to her senses out of the dreamy state when she felt two strong hands clasped her from behind and she felt warmth of breath on the back of her neck. Before she could react, turn and say anything, she experienced soft and wet kiss on the back of her neck. He touched his lips to the back of her neck at the edge of her hairs.

He felt that she trembled and squirmed in his arms. She was stunned and seemed to make feeble attempts to spring clear of him. Yet she also felt that she was thrilled from inside. Startled, she whirled around and found herself gazing deep into his eyes. His touch was indisputably arousing. She clung nearer to him. He held her close, and kissed on her forehead softly and gently. It was so wonderful and heavenly.

"This is unfair, Vinod to tiptoe from behind like this, unnoticed. Even a ghost could not have come more noiselessly," Meena blurted out with false anger, as if his stealthy ways gave her an unpleasant sensation. "You also left your boat unattended. How you can be so irresponsible and take that risk? I am not that adventurous dear," added Meena after a brief pause, feeling a little concerned and mustering enough courage to speak. The glance she gave him from her eyes was also eloquent to carry across her message."

"I have slowed the speed down and I have put it in an automatic mode, darling."

"Please do not put your desires in automatic mode like you are doing now. Be a controlled person," she mumbled, still squirming in his arms. Both hugged each other for a long time.

"It is most wonderful sail of my life. You have made this day a memorable day for me. You are so sweet," said Vinod. "If you do not believe me, my sweetheart, I can convince you with a prolonged deep kiss."

"It is okay without any proof. I believe because it is safer to believe your words. You need not convince me anymore with your adventurous activities," she retorted and laughed loudly. She would have remained indeterminately at this stage of intimacy for a long time, but she sensed that he was becoming more defiant. Blissful sensation was gradually and consistently rocketing sky ward. His eyes were glowing with eloquent appeal.

Her common sense timely whispered to her, "*Stop him, before he ventures into any more naughty defiance. You have a right to protect your own property from the devastation.*"

She realized that it is her life and she is responsible for her thoughts, emotions and actions. She became alert well before his small flames of desire attained forest fire proportion. She was now determined to regain semblance of control over the situation. She decided not to encourage his amorous advances anymore and give in to his fervent and unbridled desires.

"Tell me Vinod about your adventurous exploits in the sea," she asked smiling with insatiable curiosity. She adroitly tried to venture into safer ground and change the topic. She nestled her head in his lap after he sat in his seat taking control of his boat. He looked lovingly into her deep eyes and his exploring eyes feasted on her charming and beautiful face.

She was delighted to notice that his gaze, always so silent, now radiated geniality and love. It was revealing something magnificent within him. His fingers were, time to time, combing her hairs and removing the tresses fluttering on her radiant face. Feeling his tender care, relaxed smile played around her beautiful lips adding to her existing charm.

"Now tell me, what I asked darling."

"Sorry dear, I forgot, I was imbibing beauty of your charming face," mumbled Vinod.

"I asked about your adventurous exploits."

"Oh yes," said Vinod smiling. "It was a misty morning and I was in the deep sea, far away from shore. I heard feeble sound of some boat. Then I noticed a boat moving towards the shore. Type of the boat and its movement in the odd hours created suspicion in my mind," said Vinod, narrating the episode in detail. "I tried to contact the night patrolling party on another nearby shore. I alerted the staff and gave all the details. In the meantime, I continued following the boat from a distance."

"Wow, how interesting!" exclaimed Meena with a half suppressed smile at his obedience. She listened to him eagerly and awestruck. Her curious eyes shined with a beautiful radiance. She said nothing, but listened in utter silence with astonishment. She kept looking at him motionless, attempting in no way to break the even flow of the narrative.

"Do not you feel tense in such a situation?"

"On the other hand, I feel thrilling adventure in such scenarios," explained Vinod with a smile and tried to bring his lips nearer to her lips. She pushed his face gently away putting a finger on her lips.

"Then what happened, darling?" asked Meena, hastening to divert his direct attention. Her face flushed under his direct and admiring gaze, making her prettier.

"After some time, I heard exchange of intermittent fires. I could easily figure out that the operation had started. I was also vigilant and ready with my gun, in case the boat came back."

"I like your spirit. You are so adventurous," Meena squeaked appreciatively. "You are a real life hero."

"After some time I got a call, informing me that the boat has been intercepted and 1000 gold biscuits and 2 Kgs. of Heroin has been recovered. The officer said, 'We want your experience to locate probable hidden cavities in the boat.' I reached promptly there and helped them locate 3 hidden cavities. 500 more Gold biscuits and some electronic goods were recovered from those cavities," said Vinod with a gleam of confidence and self-esteem on his face. "I got immense job satisfaction and joy. I also got cash reward of Rupees. 5 lacs."

"How wonderful!" Meena exclaimed with fascination. "Sometimes sea is disturbed and there is lot of risk in the sea. How can you take that much risk? Do not you take some precaution to avoid risk?" said Dr. Meena with a concern.

"We have to be very alert and avoid going in the deep sea, especially when sea is disturbed. Hurricanes or cyclones are very dangerous. But I cannot help it. I want to live an adventurous life, darling. I, however, take ample precaution before going in the sea and when I am in the sea," said Vinod. "I have a wireless and mobile communication and I, constantly, keep in touch with the patrolling staff and various agencies for weather updates."

"What is generally the shape of such storms," asked she inquisitively with interest and concern. "Sometimes, they may be violent and hazardous."

"There are various types of storms, but water spouts are very dangerous."

"What are they?" asked Meena interestedly.

"Waterspouts are formed in the shape of a column of aqueous vapor from the sea to the clouds. These are thicker above and below than in the centre of the column."

"How these cyclones are caused?" she asked inquisitively.

"They are caused by electricity," explained Vinod looking deep into her eyes, combing her hairs. "They are so large that we cannot figure out their ferocity and vastness."

"Then how do you figure out its ferociousness?"

"It is only by scientific investigation that we know about their might and savagery. These whirling columns of water of different heights generally rise in clusters. They are dangerous even to big ships which come within their ambit. We can only minimize, not eliminate the risk totally," expatiated Vinod with smile looking into her eyes. "I cannot even figure out the enormity of storm hidden deep into your eyes darling."

"Yes darling. You should be alert, before it surfaces and takes you under its ambit," she laughed loudly and seductively, blinking her eyes. His conversation had a peculiar fascination for her. His knowledge of current events and general awareness was matchless. His amiable manners, ebullient adventurous spirit, which she thought very becoming in a man, endeared her profoundly.

He raised her with his arms and hugged her tight. She became alert again; before he could plant I kiss on her half open wet pink lips and promptly put finger on her lips.

"Please do not be desperate. If you really love me, please wait for a few days and let the time come. I assure you, it will be worth a wait," she whispered reassuringly with an enticing smile. Her voice sounded placid, but firm; and her eyes flashed resolution. "Do not you feel sometimes lonely in the sea? Are you really happy sailing with me today?" she said after a brief pause, adroitly trying to change the topic.

"I never feel lonely. Oceans have a voice in the waters which talks to me incessantly. Sometimes it thunders when the waves rise high and sometimes it shrieks to lure my attention," Vinod delineated. "Sometimes it rides upon the storm to show its majesty. It says far more than we could possibly comprehended," explained Vinod. "But today, when you are with me, my darling, it is whispering love, as if to divert my fervor to you. I love you darling."

"I love you too my sweetheart."

Chapter-10

It was a lovely morning. Morning tea was ready when all entered in the hall. All were well dressed and ready to start their journey to the new location for workshop. Vikas had instructed everybody to get up early in the morning and have morning tea together after getting ready.

"This is another magnificent day on this island with immense possibilities. We are going to have a wonderful time together," Vikas chimed in, with his usual smile. "Today, we are going to a splendid location, you all will love. 13 Kms. from here, there is an excellent location called 'Effervescent Falls'. We will take our breakfast and lunch there only in a natural environment and spend our whole day there," muttered Vikas with an ebullient enthusiasm. "Please carry your costumes also with you. It will be a memorable experience to take bath there, in the fall."

Cars passed through a dense forest with lush greenery and colorful wild flowers. The view was terrific. The serpentine road was, sometimes, passing through open tracts of grass land and sometimes it passed through dense jungle. The weather was lovely, the wind was perfectly still, and the air enchantingly cold but cozy.

The luxuriant water falls were visible from a distance. It was a pleasant journey and it took only 25 minutes to reach the fabulous spot. Water was falling from a very high place and the slanting sunlight passing through tiny water drops was creating a brilliant and colorful rainbow.

Everybody was flabbergasted to see such a spectacular location. Water was cascading down in torrents creating captivating view and music. They were mesmerized by the amazing scenic beauty and realized that nothing could be prettier than the scenery of the falls. The water which rushed through various fissures, collected in a natural pool, not more than 50 yards wide. Water was only chest deep and was suitable for a bath.

The wind passing through water drops was cold but assuaging. Everybody walked around and imbibed the scenic beauty and natural music emanating from falls. Sitting arrangements were made under a huge shaded tree. Everybody felt extremely happy. Breakfast table, surrounded by chairs was set in the shallow water and steaming breakfast was ready on the table. All were happy to relish breakfast in such an exotic setting.

"I hope, in this environment, we all feel abundantly enthusiastic and full of limitless energy."

"Yes, Vikas, we all feel wonderful. This is another beautiful location," mumbled Vinod, joyfully. "Your choice of this venue is also superb. We are all having memorable time together."

"We will never forget taking breakfast together in this exotic location," said Reena. "If there is a heaven on earth, this is it."

"Is there anybody who is not feeling euphoric and enthusiastic?" asked Vikas with a smile.

"I am not feeling enthusiastic," John muttered with a feeble smile, "to be frank."

"Then feel enthusiasm now in this moment by thinking enthusiastic thoughts," Vinod prompted him.

"How? Thoughts and feelings are, sometimes, not under our control."

"Why not? It is your life," retorted Vikas. "You are master of your destiny. What you think and feel should always be under your control. We all possess an abundant enthusiasm and energy. The awareness of possession of the same makes us feel jubilant. They prompt us to leap, jump, dance and sing."

"But how?" queried John with curiosity.

"It is very simple. You have many options. Just go in the open air, enjoy nature, jump, take bath in the fall, play and frolic around joyfully. You are responsible for what you think and feel. Take charge of your life," Vikas expatiated. "Do you remember, Mr. John, any situation in which you were passionate, joyful and enthusiastic?"

"Yes, I remember it in detail," John replied with elation and joy. He recalled the situation in detail. His body language changed immediately. He was no more feeling miserable now. He was instantly feeling and manifesting enthusiasm. "It was a delightful situation when I had won a major sports event. I was on the top of the hill that day. How can I forget the continuous clapping, standing ovation and the thunderous applause, which I received from my friends and the jubilant multitude?"

"Recall the situation in detail; how exactly you felt, how people reacted and how you were applauded that time. Order the same feeling now in this moment," said Vikas, smiling joyfully. "Feel it, recall it and relive it."

"Yes, now I feel blissful," chuckled John with excitement. "Recall of those situations fills me with joy. I get unlimited enthusiasm."

"If I do not feel enthusiastic in spite of our best efforts, what should I do?" asked Sofia inquisitively with curiosity.

"Fake it, till you make it," explained Vikas. "Repeat in your mind, 'I feel wonderful, ecstatic, enthusiastic, terrific and on the seventh heaven' often. Repeat it, till your subconscious takes over."

"Mind will not believe it," Sofia retorted.

"You are correct. It will not, as it is fake," explained Vikas with a smile. "But do not be disheartened and continue doing it, till you succeed. Ultimately your subconscious will believe it and will take it as real."

"Now tell me again, are you enthusiastic now, Sofia and Mr. John?" asked Vikas quizzically.

"Yes," said Sofia with a feeble smile.

"Not this way. Say loudly 'yes' with gusto and vigor, raising your hands. Everybody repeat it loudly 3 times."

Everybody repeated loudly, in unison, with vigor and energy.

"Now please stand up and come aside... Clap vigorously... It generates lot of energy. Shake and vibrate your one hand then the other... Now shake and vibrate vigorously both hands together... Do the same with your both legs raising them one by one... Now, do the same with your both legs and both the hands... of course, without raising your legs. Now sit down and relax a bit."

Vikas demonstrated the activities, as he explained. Everybody enjoyed with joy and followed his instructions.

"How far is faith helpful in creating enthusiasm?" asked Shams with desperate eagerness.

"Word, 'enthusiasm' is derived from root 'entheos' which means 'possessed by a god'," Vikas explained. "If you have faith in God, you will experience real enthusiasm."

"Okay."

"Do not suppress your enthusiasm. Share it and express it eloquently when you feel it," said Vikas delightfully. "It is infectious and it will make others also enthusiastic."

"Can anybody give some example of ordering enthusiastic feelings?" asked Vikas, pointing at Sofia. "Sofia, do you want to say something?"

"Once I was stuck in a traffic jam, while returning from Shimla. All were annoyed and blowing horns incessantly in desperation. Some continued sitting in their cars and some came out and started shouting obscenities," Sofia narrated the instance. "One old couple, in the meantime, alighted from a car putting their stereo at full volume and started dancing. Almost everybody, most of them honeymoon couples, came out and started dancing with full enthusiasm and vigor."

"Wow!" exclaimed Mitali. "Enthusiasm is really infectious."

"All were in blissful mood and danced joyfully," added Sofia. "That day I realized that we can live joyfully just by changing our way of thinking and readjusting our attitude. Whenever I am in a traffic jam or I feel gloomy, I recall that situation, order the same feeling and feel delightful."

Everybody listened in silence, motionless and flabbergasted.

"Thank you very much for the wonderful example," said Vikas encouragingly. "I feel that such real life stories are very stimulating, uplifting and motivating. They constantly remain in our subconscious mind and motivate us enormously when we are gloomy, depressed or miserable."

"You all have unlimited enthusiasm. You are much more powerful, creative and effective than you think. Do not let your enthusiasm subside. With enthusiasm, you had done wonderful things, earlier in your life. Order the same feeling again, here and now," reiterated Vikas. "Right now, you have tremendous power to do amazing things and create anything you like. Step ahead and put your enthusiasm to use."

"Any more stories from anybody?" asked Vikas inquisitively.

Nobody buzzed.

"Before we proceed for bath and lunch, I will like to reiterate a few points and recapitulate what we have discussed about the topic," said Vikas. "If you just force yourself to act enthusiastic, you will certainly become more enthusiastic. To become enthusiastic, therefore, act more enthusiastic, even if you are actually not. Fake it till you make it. You should define your destination. If you don't know where you are going, you will move like a rudderless boat and ultimately you will end up somewhere else. One man asked an old man, 'Which road I should take?'

'First tell me, where do you want to go?'

'I do not know.'

'Then take any road,' said the old man with a smile."

"First define your goals and then decide what you need to do to achieve them. Draw strength from the positives. Learn from the times you failed, but focus and draw inspiration from your previous successes. Look for "Aha!" moments, expatiated Vikas in detail. "Write them on a paper and paste at a place where you can refer to them often. Don't dwell on the negatives. Stop worrying about things you can't change. Make a list of the things you are grateful for and make a list of things that make you happy."

"You all look tired. Is not it?" asked Vikas.

"Yes," said Reena contorting her mouth in a feeble smile, with a sigh. "We need a break now."

"We will have lunch, but after bath in the fall," said Vikas. "You are all well-equipped, so go and get ready."

"I will not feel comfortable taking bath like this," mumbled Reena. "I do not have suitable dress also."

"It is up to you to choose between comfort and a memorable thrill," said Sofia. "It is going to be an outstanding experience to take bath here; you will always relish its memory. It is my personal experience, because I have taken bath many times earlier in this natural pool."

"I have an extra dress. You may take from me," said Mitali with a charming smile nodding at Reena.

"Okay, I will also take bath," said Reena.

It was a marvelous experience to frolic around in chest-deep cold water and under fall. Tiny cold droplets were creating fantastic sensation in body. By that time lunch was ready on tables.

"Take your own time," said Vikas. "There is no hurry."

Lunch was served on the table, under a huge tree, whose thick branches came down close to the ground. The food was very delectable, hot and aromatic. The curry was prepared from local wild herbs.

The ambience was soothing and magnificent. It was an exotic and exquisite experience to take lunch in this magnificent natural surroundings. This place was so placid and secluded; there seemed a magic circle drawn about that mysterious and serene place, shutting out the outer world.

Everybody enjoyed delicious food.

"I hope everybody is back," said Vikas.

"Yes, everybody is here," all muttered and nodded in unison.

"Are you all happy?" asked Vikas.

"Yes, very happy," said all.

"Then there is no need to discuss happiness which I was going to do," said Vikas guffawing. "You all know how to be happy."

Everybody laughed exuberantly.

"Happiness is such a vast subject, we can discuss it for years together," explained Vikas. "It has different meaning for different persons. According to Harrison Ford; *'Being happy is something you have to learn. I often surprise myself by saying "Wow, this is it. I guess I'm happy. I got a home I love. A career that I love. I'm even feeling more and more at peace with myself." If there's something else to happiness, let me know. I'm ambitious for that, too.'* We can all be happy and achieve happiness any time."

"How can I achieve happiness?" asked Reena inquisitively, impelled by an unendurable curiosity.

"You should keep a few points in mind," elucidated Vikas. "Being happy or unhappy is a matter of choice. It is our attitude that makes us feel happy or unhappy. We face all types of situations during the day, and some of them may not be conducive to happiness. We can choose to obsess about the unhappy events or relish the joyful moments. I will take up these pints one by one and discuss in detail."

"You cannot be happy in past and future. Omar Khayyam used to say, *"Be happy for this moment. This moment is your life."* Appreciate and relish every moment and take from it everything that you possibly can. Be happy now in this moment. Manifest your best and do your best," expounded Vikas further. "You are capable of achieving success and happiness, now, in this moment. Smile, laugh, relax and be happy, now."

"Very interesting indeed. Tell me more about the ways to achieve happiness," asked Sofia, interestedly.

"You tell me," shot back Vikas with a wide grin. "This is an interactive workshop."

"I think it is making others happy," Sofia asserted. "We can make others happy by helping them, by maintaining congenial relationship in office and family. We get real happiness, when we put smile on others face. It gives lasting peace and satisfaction to make others happy."

"Yes, you are correct," said Vikas, with a smile. "Helping others makes you instantly happy and joyful. Mahatma Gandhi correctly said: *'Happiness depends upon what you give, not on what you can receive.'* Put, therefore a smile on others face to achieve real happiness."

"We do not often get such opportunities," mumbled Sofia.

"There are so many, if you have passion to help. You can also create such opportunities, even if they are not there," Dr. Meena interposed. "Visit a hospital or a nursing home in your vicinity and care for needy and sick persons. You can also offer financial help, attention and time to needy persons and poor patients."

"Thank you, Dr. Meena," said Sofia.

"You may help and care for old and handicapped people living without families on the streets. Do each day at least one act of kindness to help others make them happy. You can say a kind word to an acquaintance, help your colleagues. You can also stop your car at the crossroad to let people cross, give your seat in a bus to someone else, or give a small present to someone. There are so many ways to make others happy and be happy," added Vikas. "They will love you for just showing up and having conversation with them... Mr. John, do you want to say something?"

"Yes, please let me add here; it is my personal experience that real happiness is achieved when you put smile on others face and make others happy," said John. "One day I visited a hospital in my area to give food to needy patients. I gave food to two patients lying on separate beds. While giving sweets after giving food, one patient asked me, 'Please give both the sweets to my friend, here, on this bed. It is his birthday and I do not have any gift to give him.' I was impressed and I gave 2 extra pieces to both and distributed sweet to other patients also to celebrate his birthday. All were happy and I was the happiest person."

"It is a very good example, Mr. John. I remember an expression from Mark Twain: *'The best way to cheer yourself up is to try to cheer somebody else up.'* Now you tell me, Mr. John, how we can achieve happiness?" asked Vikas after a pause.

"You do not require much to be happy. Abraham Lincoln used to say, *'most folks are about as happy as they make up their minds to be. Happiness is from within; it is not a matter of externals.'* happiness is in simplicity. If you have bread and butter, things to wear and roof on your head, you do not require plenty of money to be happy," explained John. "Superfluous wealth is spent on superfluities only."

"You are correct. You can get happiness in small and things and simple mundane activities," said Vikas. "Focus on whatever you are doing. Smile when you wake up. Visualize all the good things that are going to happen today. Visualize a wonderful day ahead. Commit random, spontaneous acts of kindness to make others happy. If you do something without being found out, it will be even better."

"Okay, let us do some more brainstorming and find out a few more simple ways to be happy. We will do some practical exercises also. It is turn of Dr. Meena to add some more points."

"I agree with you that happiness very much depends on simple things. Telephone and ask someone how he is… send flowers and offer help… do simple acts of kindness in day-to-day life," said Dr. Meena. "You can do a few more simple activities to add to your personal happiness. Take a cold bath or an occasional hot bath… get a massage, swim… and play game for rejuvenating and relaxing your body and mind… Exercise and powerwalk regularly, as physical activity gets your body rejuvenated and it also helps you get into good mood… Go out and get sunshine and fresh air."

"Thank you, Dr. Meena… Do you want to say something, Reena?" Vikas nodded at her.

"Yes, Vikas. Invite someone and cook a lovely meal for him," said Reena. "Give and exchange smile. Tell a joke and laugh together."

"Do not forget me Reena when you cook something special… Mr. Shams," Vikas prompted, gesticulating at him with a smile, "will you like to say something?"

"Spend time with friends and relatives and have fun," Shams chirped. "Have a sense of humor… Laugh and smile to make your mood better… Watch your favorite movies… Listen to music as the right song can remove negativity… Dance and sing… Be innovative and break your personal rules, sometimes."

"Give a gift to someone. Help somebody and not get found out. It is win-win for both. He gets the joy of receiving and you get the joy of giving. Join a social networking group," interjected Mitali raising her hand. "Express your emotion. Let your emotions out in loud way possible… Call a friend, he will cheer you up… Start a blog or a project… Being busy with something you enjoy is a prime source of happiness."

"Vinod, do you want to say something?" asked Vinod noting his gesticulations.

"Yes. Sorry to interrupt again. I have found that meditation also helps. Take a nap or practice deep relaxing breathing. If all else fails, fall asleep. Even if you sleep for 20 minutes, you will feel relaxed and peaceful," interjected

Vinod. "To add a few more points; Praise someone publicly. He will feel happy. When you give happiness to others, you get more of it."

"Can you prove your point by giving a living example?" asked Vikas with a smile.

Vinod felt uneasy to face an unexpected question. He groped for the suitable words to continue even flow of narrative. He soon regained his composure and started speaking again with a beaming smile, "Dr. Meena is a gorgeous young lady, with so many assets," said Vinod with a wide grin. "She is doing tremendous service to humanity. She is a marvelous creation of God."

"Vinod is a wonderful, adventurous and handsome guy," Meena interrupted with her usual charming smile, reciprocating his praise. "He is doing more that he is paid for. He is enriching exchequer by risking his life."

Everybody laughed.

"See, how infectious praise is," Vikas chuckled guffawing. "You all have seen, his praise is immediately reciprocated. Praise creates a chain reaction and instant reciprocation. This chain reaction spreads around joy and happiness."

"There are a few more simple activities which you can do to create happiness and be happy," interpose Sofia. "Listen to others with interest and attention. Listen more than you talk. Let others speak. Be there when people are in need. Send a 'thank you' note, an e-mail or flowers."

"Give a free angel hug and say, '*I love you with my whole heart unconditionally, as you are.*' Repeat it till your subconscious takes over," Reena chimed in with a charming smile, participating zestfully in the lively discussion.

"Let us give this idea a practical shape, now, in this moment," Vikas instructed. "Stand up, everybody and choose a random partner... I mean it... Do it now... Hug your partner."

Everybody followed his instructions and he also did as he suggested.

"Now, look into the eyes of your partner and repeat the sentence, Reena has suggested, 5 times," said Vikas in a jubilant mood.

Everybody repeated: '*I love you with my whole heart unconditionally, as you are.*'

"Very good," said Vikas. "Let us continue brainstorming. Mitali, it is your turn."

"Dance, like nobody is watching and sing, as if nobody is listening." said Mitali.

"Stand up everybody again. Let us dance for 5 minutes," said Vikas. "You will eliminate boredom and feel joyful and rejuvenated."

Everybody stood up and danced joyfully.

"Just feel happy. Even if you are not joyful, fake it till you make it. Practice it now," said Vikas and elucidated with demonstrating. "Put a pencil between your lips parallel to lips. This will shape your lips into a smile. Practice this also now."

"Attitude also plays an important role to make us happy," said Vikas. "If you have a positive and joyful attitude, you will be happy. Here I want to quote Martha Washington: '*I am still determined to be cheerful and happy, in whatever situation I may be; for I have also learned from experience that the greater part of our happiness or misery depends upon our dispositions, and not upon our circumstances.*' What happens may not be in your hand, but how you react to the situation is always in your hand."

"Happiness depends, primarily, on your attitude. Endeavor to change the way you look at the things. Always look at the brighter side of the situation. Do not let your mind drag you to think about negativity and intricacy in any situation," Vikas expatiated further. "Look at the positive side of every situation. You can choose and attract happiness in every situation."

"One person was asked the reason for his happiness. He said, 'It is very simple. When I get up early in the morning, I have two choices, either to be happy or to be unhappy. Obviously, I opt for being happy. This choice has made all the difference in my life.' Attitude makes lot of difference; positive attitude gives happiness and negative attitude gives us pain," Vikas elaborated further. Everybody listened in silence, motionless, endeavoring in no way to break the unfluctuating flow of the narrative.

"We can be happy in all situations, because it is our attitude that makes us feel happy or unhappy," reiterated Vikas. "It is your attitude and reaction to the problem, which makes significant difference. Now I want to ask you a question. What will happen, if you boil potatoes in one pot, eggs in the second pot, and tea in the third pot separately?" asked Vikas after a pause.

"The egg will become hard, potatoes will become soft," Sofia replied, "and coffee will make water colorful."

"All the three items faced the same fire, but they reacted differently. Similarly, if you have a positive attitude and react in constructive manner, you will get colorful results," explained Vikas. "Do not let events spoil your mood, otherwise you will become slave and lose your freedom. Reaction to what happens is always in your hand."

"We can choose to be happy in any situation in our lives," explained Vikas. "According to Jimmy Dean: *I can't change the direction of the wind, but I can adjust my sails to always reach my destination.*' Adjust the sail, therefore, and move ahead resolutely with a positive mental attitude towards your cherished destination."

"I have a relevant and funny joke about attitude to share, if you allow me," John interposed smiling.

"Yes… Please… Go ahead," Vikas encouraged him with a smile. "Every remark, quote, statement or assertions, which makes us happy is welcome. We must have a profound sense of humor to live a joyful life. Humor gives lot of happiness, especially when shared with others."

John said, "*One day I found a friend of mine gloomy and miserable. I asked him, "What is problem and why are you so dejected?*

He said, "My wife has an affair with someone else."

One day, I found him very happy and asked, "Why this change? Is affair of your wife over?"

"No, I changed my attitude, instead," said he.

"How did the change in attitude help?" I asked him.

"Earlier I worried that she is my wife and she is having an affair with someone else. Now I think she is and has always been that person's girlfriend and she is now having an affair with me."

"Wow… Great…!" exclaimed Mitali laughing. Everybody laughed joyfully. "We can readjust the sail and attitude and give humorous turn to our problems and enjoy life."

"Wonderful joke John, thanks," said Vikas. "There is a quotation by William Arthur Ward: *'The pessimist complains about the wind; the optimist expects it to change; the realist adjusts the sails.'* Readjust, therefore, your attitude and live joyfully."

"Faith and gratitude also makes us happy," said Reena. "An attitude of gratitude is a powerful contributor to a happy life. We must, therefore, make the best use of what we have and enjoy what God have given us. We must express our gratitude to Almighty for so many of his blessings."

"Thanks Reena for your contribution to brainstorming session. We get lot of peace and happiness, if we have faith in God and express gratitude to Almighty. God has sent us here in this world and is always with us. He never leaves us alone. He answers our prayers in various ways," explained Vikas. "It may be the single most effective way to increase happiness. Gratitude walk, which we had practiced that day, is a solution in such a situation."

"We got so many suggestions to be happy," said Vikas. "Shams, can you also suggest some more ways to be happy and joyful?"

"Unconditional love gives a real joy. It gives us an opportunity to help others and maintain enduring relationships. Love, therefore, unconditionally to live a joyful life. I think, loving yourself and others gives lot of pleasure and bliss," said Shams. "Kristin Chenoweth has correctly said: *'If you can learn to love yourself and all the flaws, you can love other people so much better. And that makes you so happy.'* Do not envy people who are happy. On the contrary, be happy for their happiness."

"Optimism also plays an important role to make us happy and joyful," interjected Vinod. "Always expect happiness in all situations. Do your best, be your best, manifest your best and hope for the best. Optimists are able to cope with the life situations in healthier manner. They take failures and setbacks with a grain of salt and do not let them ruin their self-confidence or self-esteem."

"Yes, fantastic suggestions, Vinod and Shams," said Vikas. "Rabindra Nath Tagore expressed: *'I have become my own version of an optimist. If I can't make it through one door, I'll go through another door - or I'll make a door.*

Something terrific will come no matter how dark the present.'
Be, therefore, a tough-minded Dynamic optimist and live
joyfully."

"An optimist looks at a challenge as an opportunity to
grow. He is more creative and works smarter and harder
for positive results," explained Vikas. "They are always
even-tempered, serene and calm in face of difficulties. This
attitude makes them blissful and happy."

"Optimists are not afraid of unknown. They accept the
reality, do what they can, and move on. They make the best
of their journey, before reaching their desired destination.
For them, it is better to travel hopefully than to arrive. They
get lasting peace and happiness by following these noble
ideas and putting them into practice… Dr. Meena, can you
add some more points here?"

"Optimists see brighter possibilities, silver linings and
happier endings in every situation and they are adroit in
finding creative solutions in every situation," said Dr. Meena.

"Thanks, Dr. Meena. We should be tough-minded
dynamic optimists. We should be dynamic enough to take
charge of our feelings, thoughts and actions," said Vikas.
"Take an effective action with optimism in this moment,
free from anger and guilt, and at the same time remain
joyful and relaxed by releasing all tension and stress."

"I remember a very good quotation by Louise L. Hay:
*'You are not a helpless victim of your own thoughts, but rather
a master of your mind. What do you need to let go of? Take
a deep breath, relax, and say to yourself, 'I am willing to let
go. I release. I let go. I release all tension. I release all fear. I
release all anger. I release all guilt. I release all sadness. I let
go of all old limitations. I let go, and I am at peace. I am at
peace with myself. I am at peace with the process of life. I am
safe.'* Optimism is not enough, be a tough-minded dynamic

optimist. Do not think we require discussing this topic anymore, as we had discussed it earlier also."

"Now we will discuss role of Yoga and relaxation for living stress-free life," Vikas broke in. "Try to be relaxed, happy, stress-free and serene all the time. A stressful environment can have an adverse impact on all aspects of your life, be it work, your love life or your relationships. It can affect the way you function in your day-to-day life. But fortunately with some precaution we can easily get rid of stress."

"There are unexpected problems in our day-to-day life. We have to tackle them," said John.

"Tackle them with a positive mental attitude. Be solution oriented and solve them with faith and hope. Take effective steps with an effortless ease to solve the problem. If faced with an unexpected problem affirm, '*It is not a problem, but a challenge, an opportunity to show your best and to learn the overdue knowledge, law and procedures. Do not label it as stressful, but an amazing learning experience*," elaborated Vikas. "Sit relaxed and close your eyes."

"Why to close eyes all the time, while relaxing?" asked Mitali laughing. "How does it help?"

"Closing eyes stops dissipation of energy," replied Vikas. "If you do not like to close your eyes, you can, very well, opt for partial closure. You will have the same benefits. As soon as dissipation starts, you will be able to observe and take corrective action."

"Thanks, Vikas," said Mitali.

"Take an easy deep breath, keeping your body totally relaxed. Continue doing it for a few minutes," Vikas instructed further. "While inhaling, imagine you are taking in joy, peace, gratitude and while exhaling you are releasing anger, worry and stress."

Everybody followed his instructions.

"Dr. Meena, are you relaxed?"

"Not completely," said Meena. "I feel some tension in some body parts."

"Be aware and focused, take up one part. Strain that part, while inhaling and release the stress, while exhaling. Then shift your attention to another stressed part and repeat the same process. Everybody, please do the same," said Vikas. "Now tell me, how you feel."

"Much better," said Dr. Meena. "It is quite effective. Please tell me in detail, which factors cause stress and how to effectively control it. Stress is very harmful for our body and mind."

"Worry is the main culprit. I am coming to your request soon," said Vikas. "Decide not to worry about anything in any kind of circumstances."

"But worry solves so many problems," said Sofia.

"No, it never solves a problem," blurted out Vikas, "but it further aggravates it. Thinking of solutions and taking an effective action, solves many problems. Be aware and watch your thoughts. Whenever you catch yourself worrying and thinking negative thoughts, start thinking of pleasant things. Think of solutions and take effective actions. Analyze what is problem, what is the cause of the problem, what are solutions and what is best solution. After analysis start taking action."

"Thanks, Vikas," said Sofia.

"Listen to relaxing, uplifting music," added Vikas. "Start a favorite music and start dancing. Music and dance are very effective stress busters. See it for yourself."

He put on music on his lap top and exhorted all to stand and dance. Everybody danced in jubilant mood.

"Each day, devote some time to reading a few pages of an inspiring book or article. Smile and laugh more often and watch funny comedies that make you laugh," explained Vikas. "Associate with happy people, and try to learn from them to be happy. Remember, happiness is contagious. When you are happy, stress evaporates."

"Thanks Vikas. Let me add here a few more points. Getting up early and planning day ahead helps a lot," interjected Meena. "When we rise early, we have sufficient time for exercise in natural environment. We can easily accomplish our daily chores in a stress-free manner. We do not have to run to office with a frenzied speed. Traffic is also less in the early hours."

"Thanks Dr. Meena," said Vikas. "Inaction also causes problems. It results in pile up of unfinished work, which causes stress. When we act, we are bound to commit a few mistakes. We should take mistakes for granted and continue taking actions. If we take more action, there will be fewer mistakes and there will be less stress. We should, neither blow our mistakes out of proportion, nor perceive failures. We should concentrate, instead on positive actions, accomplishments and results."

"Does anybody want to ask question on the topic under discussion?"

Nobody responded.

Chapter-11

John was in habit of getting up early in the morning so that the day is started without any haste and morning chores are completed joyfully, with effortless ease. Today also, as usual, he got up early and opened his window. Soft spring air, full of the freshness of young leaves, and mingled with the sea breeze entered his room to brush his face. He felt blissful and immensely rejuvenated. The memory of his last visit to hills with Mitali was still fresh in his mind. He was dreaming of another visit with her to spend some lovely time with her. He decided to request Mitali to visit the beach in the afternoon.

The workshop finished a bit earlier and everybody was free to spend his evening in his own way. John slowed down and gesticulated at Mitali to walk to him. She was already looking at him fondly with her usual smile. She responded by walking nearer to him.

"You might be tired, honey, after a hectic day schedule," mumbled John with concern. "How was the day?"

"Like other days, this day was also wonderful. I enjoyed every minute of this day," said Mitali with her charming smile. "Your presence, love and care have made it even more magnificent. I am lucky to get a marvelous friend like you."

"Thank you Mitali," chuckled John happily with a smile, looking into her eyes.

"What are you planning to do in the evening?"

"Nothing special; why? Tell me, if you have something in your mind," murmured Mitali, looking at him with her loving glances.

"What about going for an outing?"

"Wow, it is a beautiful proposal," Mitali chimed in. "I was also thinking to spend some time with you."

"Okay, get fresh and get ready. I will pick you up," John chuckled joyfully.

"Where do you plan to go darling?" asked Mitali.

"What about visiting nearby sea beach?"

"How wonderful!" Mitali exclaimed. "I love sea beaches."

"Then go, get fresh and get ready fast," John advised her in a joyful mood. "Wait for me."

No one else was there at the beach this time. The weather was moist but quite pleasing. They sat down on the sand and relaxed at the solitary beach. The sea breeze was quite refreshing. She nestled her head in his lap, while John combed her hairs with his fingers softly. Both felt wonderful sitting on the beach.

"I feel joyous in your company," said Mitali. "I wish I had met you earlier."

Blazing heat had, by now, subsided to a considerable extent, but there was still enough warmth in the sun. The assuaging warm breeze worked its soporific magic. It gradually soothed her and gently relaxed her tensed muscles. Her body relaxed completely after taking a short nap in his lap. She remained in the dreamy state, half asleep, till she heard cry of seagulls in distance.

"I hope you are fresh now, after taking a soothing nap," mumbled John with a smile. "Will you like to go in the sea and take bath?"

"Yes, darling."

"Okay let us go," said John. They looked around. There was nobody else to see them. Also, there was no possibility for anybody else to come on the beach. In a jiffy, Mitali slipped into the water. John joined her forthwith. They swam silently and blessedly for a long time. He was worried to see her going deeper. He admonished her not to go farther in the deep sea. She ignored him and continued moving ahead. He swam faster to catch her and bring her back.

"What are you doing? We are not very good swimmers. There is no one else here to rescue us. Do you want to drown both of us?" John yelled. He made an impulsive surge forward, grabbed her in his arms, pulled her to his heart, and covered her face with incessant kisses, before he perceived her condition. "We should not take risk."

"Sorry darling," she said hugging him with a tight embrace. "It was a wonderful experience to frolic around in the water. I could not resist my temptation."

"Do not you notice the huge waves of up to one meter height are crashing on the beach?" John admonished her, "Sea is a bit rough and we have to be careful."

They both felt rejuvenated and fresh after taking bath. To their utter astonishment, a big fish jumped out of water and fell in the hands of John. He yelled joyously and caught hold of the same with help of Mitali. Then they moved ashore, holding the fish in their hands with help of each other.

"What a wonderful experience," squeaked John. He appeared ecstatic with tremendous bliss. "I never expected it. This is the second best, serendipitous catch of my life."

"What is this 'serendipitous'."

"It is unexpected euphoric gain," John mumbled with delight, wrapping the fish carefully in a towel.

"And which was your first catch?" said Mitali, entering again in the water, holding his hand.

"Let the time come," whispered John with a butter-soft voice. "I will tell you, my sweetheart."

"No, please tell me now," she insisted, coming closer to him, looking deep into his eyes. She came so close, he could experience her enhanced heartbeats and warm breaths. "We are close friends. Are not we? You should not keep anything secret from me." Her eyes looked at him incessantly, with a questioning expectant look.

"It is you, my sweetheart," John jested with jubilation. He glanced at her with a romantic look. He lifted her torso with both the hands and hugged her. She slid arms and draped them around him and rose on her toes to get closer to him to get a tighter hug. She clung tightly to him, as if she wanted thrilling excitement to continue forever.

"I love you sweetie. I never had such a feeling for anybody else in my life," John whispered with a butter-soft voice, hauling her closer.

Listening to his adoring words, a shiver of a strange irresistible joy ran through her. Her lips were agape with a pleasant surprise. She was ecstatic to hear his words and she believed what he said. She also frantically searched her mind and asked herself, "*Do I also love him?*"

"I also love you, darling," she managed to utter.

As soon as he could put his lips on her half open lips, a huge wave swept them down. He fell on her. Both stood up, as wave passed.

"I wrongly thought that there is absolutely no distraction on this solitary beach," squeaked John guffawing with hilarity.

"Have patience my sweetheart. It means time is not yet ripe for your naughty intentions," Mitali chuckled. "Wait for appropriate time, sweetie."

"How long will I have to wait?"

"Everything happens in God's own time. Release your passionate desires to the universe and wait," said Mitali laughing loudly with hilarity. "Let God decide what, when, and where you get."

"Do you really love me?"

"Yes, I love you with my whole heart. But we do not know much about each other yet, darling," Mitali muttered with her butter-soft voice. "You do not know about my past. I believe in sincere relationship. There are some dark patches in my life, of which you are not aware. I want to reveal those dark spots to you, before you arrive at some decision. I want to confess something, before we leap ahead."

"Do not hesitate. Feel free to discuss anything you like. We are good friends, are not we?" said John.

"Yes, we are," said Mitali. "A few memories still haunt me, even after I have attended so many workshops."

"Were these workshops not helpful?"

"Of course, they were helpful to some extent. My hurt feelings were assuaged," said Mitali despondently, "after attending such workshops."

He came closer to her, wiped her streaming eyes with his hanky and hugged her softly.

"Tell me everything in detail, dear."

She realized that it was a proper time to apprise him about the past.

"I was sexually abused in my adolescent years," Mitali asserted and started narration of the incident. He listened to her with undivided silent attention, without disrupting her narrative.

He was shocked to listen to her narrative, but recovered fast. He encouraged her to express her pent-up feelings, heard her words with a resolute composure. She explained in detail, what happened and how it happened.

On her ceasing to speak, he stood up spreading his arms. Both hugged each other for a long time. A shiver of ecstasy ran through her. She congratulated herself to express herself properly, eloquently and boldly, in the midst of her bewilderment.

"Take it easy, God is always with you. He takes care of everything," he assured her with a soft assuaging voice. "It was not your fault, was it?"

"No."

"Can you change past?"

"No."

"Life exists in the present moment. Make your dwelling place in 'now'," said John. "Today is a new day. Make the best of it. Never feel miserable in your life. You are a bold lady. In spite of all this, you are successful lady and you reached your pinnacle."

"I still feel remnants of anger and frustration," said Mitali. "Those agonizing memories creep in, time to time, and haunt me."

"It is natural. Do not forget that you are a strong lady. I have a firm belief that you can, very well, take charge of your life," said John. "Fix one-to-one session with Vikas. I am sure, he will assuage your feelings and eliminate them forever from your psyche."

"You have already relieved my melancholy to a considerable extent, John. I will discuss with Vikas also in one-to-one session. He will also help me, I am sure, eliminate the remaining traces of trauma from my mind," said Mitali with a feeble smile. "Do you still love me?"

"A past event cannot shake or mitigate my present love, as in my love; there is a stronger basis than mere crush or sexual lure. Our unconditional love will not be wavered by time or circumstances. I love you without any string attached. I love you unconditionally," said John with lovely smile, putting his hand on her shoulder.

"I love you too my sweetheart from the core of my heart," quipped Mitali joyfully. "I am lucky to have you in my life. Your presence in my life has made a lot of difference."

Chapter-12

Mitali was tired. She took a fashion magazine and flipped through it in the bed, till she felt sleepy. She did not know when she slept. It was a non-stop relaxing sleep. She woke up quite early in the morning, hearing chirping of birds outside. Her body woke with a glimmering consciousness. She was feeling fresh as a chicken, when it comes out of an egg into a new universe. She opened window to let the fresh air come in. She felt fresh and blissful. The birds were whistling incessantly and flapping their wings, as if to welcome the morning. It was still dark outside.

It was another exquisite day. Mitali was happy that she was going to meet Vikas in the evening, on the terrace of the resort building. She was always motivated, whenever she spent time with Vikas. She had, earlier also, attended the workshops organized by Vikas, but this was very special. She was very happy to come to this resort and attend this workshop.

She was enormously benefitted by attending such workshops, but some painful memories still lingered in her memory to stress her psyche incessantly. She was happy, she boldly discussed her despondency with John and she was greatly relieved to get his positive response. She was eager to discuss this problem with Vikas. John had also advised her to discuss the problem with Vikas. She otherwise also, liked Vikas and always felt very comfortable in his company. She had wonderful time with him earlier also on various occasions.

They reached on the terrace and sat together in veranda. There were so many flower pots replete with fragrant flowers. Smell of her perfume blended with fragrance of flowers to create a wonderful aromatic feel. She looked beautiful in light violet sari and matching blouse.

Waiter brought tea. The waiter was very attentive, and poured water in the glasses and asked, if they would like him to pour the tea also for them.

"Yes, please do it," said Mitali smiling.

"Please push the call bell and let me know, if you want some more tea or coffee, anytime," said waiter.

"Okay, we will let you know, in case we want something. Thank you very much," said Vikas.

"You look so fresh, cute and lovely. Dress plays an important role in uplifting the mood. Your dressing sense is superb. You know how to look your best," said Vikas smiling.

"Thanks Vikas," Mitali chimed in with her usual joyful smile.

Both liked and enjoyed the verdant setting. They relished tea, just sitting and looking at each other. There was only a peaceful silence, except a few desultory words, they uttered time to time. Her face was changing colors and Vikas was quietly observing the metamorphosis.

"You are a magnificent young lady and melancholy does not suit your gorgeous face," said Vikas with a smile, trying to pierce her gloom, putting his hand on her shoulder. "Look at me and smile."

She smiled, looking into his eyes.

"Yes, it looks better," said Vikas with his usual lovely smile. "Now tell me what bothers you, Mitali? Tell me everything in detail."

"I was born in a poor family. My father expired, when I was only 12 years old. I had to leave my existing house along with my mother and brother. My father's friend gave me shelter. We started living in the servant's quarter and my mother helped his family in domestic work," said Mitali, taking a deep sigh.

"Okay, go ahead," Vikas prompted her. "Please sit more comfortably and take a few relaxing breaths."

"One day my mother had gone to market. He entered in my house. He appeared to be inebriated. He caught hold of me and tried to force himself upon me. I could smell his intentions and shouted for help…" Mitali mumbled, downheartedly. Vikas took out his handkerchief and wiped her streaming eyes.

"Shouted for help…," Vikas prompted her.

"He had closed the door. I struggled hard to thwart his amorous advances and at the same time, I continued screaming with full force."

"You are a bold and pious lady," said Vikas, encouraging her.

"I was lucky, his wife heard my screams and came running to my quarter for my rescue," Mitali narrated with gloomy demeanor. "She helped me a lot to regain my composure and said sorry for her husband's obnoxious behavior. She was a very helpful lady. She rehabilitated us in Mumbai."

"Have you been living in Mumbai since then?" asked Vikas with concern. "How is his family life?"

"His wife was unhappy with him. She could not pull along with him and she dumped him and came to Mumbai. She is living in my area nowadays. She has her own house there and she is living a comfortable life. I extend her all possible help. She is just like my local guardian and very caring."

"Where is her husband now?" asked Vikas inquisitively.

"He is also very much changed now. His business is now in a bad shape. He tried to request his wife to go back with him, but she refused. He came to me also to say sorry, but I did not respond and asked him to go away, not to come back again," said Mitali. "Memory of what happened that day still haunts me."

"Was he really sorry for what he had done?" asked Vikas curiously.

"Yes, I think so," she mumbled after thinking for a moment.

"Did you try to forgive him?"

"I had tried when you had encouraged me in a workshop in Bombay, but could not succeed that time."

"Do you want to get rid of this trauma?"

"Yes, I want to be free from it," said Mitali. "I will do anything you suggest."

"Okay. I know and believe that you can do it," affirmed Vikas reassuringly. "You have tremendous courage. God has given you sufficient strength to forgive others and yourself."

"Thank you, Vikas," said Mitali with a feeble smile. "Your encouragement and trust makes me more enthusiastic and bold."

"I can encourage you to manifest only what is within you," said Vikas reassuringly, "and, I very well know, you have the requisite strength. You are a unique creation of God and you are here for a splendid purpose in this world. You have to live with gusto and enthusiasm."

"Thank you Vikas."

"Please relax and ease these wrinkles on your forehead," said Vikas with a smile, touching softly her forehead with tips of his fingers. "Sit more comfortably... close your eyes and take a few deep breaths... Do it now... yes... like this... continue till you feel totally relaxed."

She followed his instructions.

"Relaxed deep breathing is an instant guard against stress. Always practice a peaceful and relaxed breathing, if you feel stress is beginning to take hold," explained Vikas, readjusting her posture. "Your senses will respond more efficiently, if you are relaxed."

"Release the tension in every part of your body. Feel at ease and peaceful," explained Vikas. "Inhale slowly and deeply for count of 5, hold for the count of 3 and exhale completely for the count of 5. Repeat for a few times, till you feel relaxed."

"How do you feel now?" asked Vikas looking at her with concern after a pause.

"I feel serene and calm," said Mitali with composed demeanor. "I feel relaxed."

"Very good. Continue relaxed breathing. While inhaling, imagine that you are breathing in joy, forgiveness, unconditional love, peace and relaxation; and while exhaling, you are releasing stress, resentment, hate, tension and unease. Ease every part of your body, one by one and relax. If you still notice stress in any part of your body, stretch that part, while inhaling and release, while exhaling. Keep your eyes closed and continue doing it, as long as you feel comfortable."

"How much relaxed do you feel now?"

"I feel now totally relaxed, as if I am in a pre-sleep 'Alfa' stage."

"Keep your eyes closed. Now your mind is responding to my suggestions. Your mind is under your control. It is as serene and placid as a deep lake."

"Yes," Mitali mumbled in a butter-soft voice in dreamy state.

"Now repeat with me: 'I am serene and calm… I am responsible for my thoughts, feelings and actions… I am master of my destiny… It is my life and I am in driving seat of my life… God has given me power to forgive… It is within my power to forgive myself and others," said Vikas slowly. Mitali repeated every word, as if in a dreamy state.

"Now relax again. Take a few deep breaths and keep your body and mind relaxed. Now imagine Mr… is sitting in front of you," said Vikas.

"Ease these grimaces," said Vikas, again putting his hand on her forehead. "Take it easy."

"Okay."

"Now repeat: 'Today… now… in this moment… I forgive you with my whole heart Mr…. totally. There is no resentment against you in my mind now… I release you and make you free this moment… I also forgive myself and release myself from all stress and guilt'," said Vikas with slow pace. "Feel that all tension is evaporating into air like a dark cloud… Now, the cloud has totally disappeared… ambience is clear and everything appears bright."

She followed his instructions and did what she was advised.

"Repeat: 'from today onward, I am free and you are free. Life is too important to be wasted on resentments and guilt," said Vikas. "Now, relax for a few minutes and take stock of the situation… Now, you can open your eyes."

"Tell me how you feel now." said Vikas smiling brightly. "Could you successfully forgive him?"

"Yes, Vikas, this time I could do it successfully. Thank you very much," she squeaked with a charming smile.

"I noticed that after a few twitches and grimaces your face was relaxed. And when your face is relaxed you look more charming," chuckled Vikas with a wonderful smile.

"Really?" she said smiling more profusely with a charming smile.

"Tell me Mitali, what exactly did you feel?"

"In the beginning, while recalling the situation, I felt very tense. I was becoming out of control. Here, relaxed breathing and your assuaging touch of my forehead helped a lot. Having been relaxed, my body and mind worked more efficiently. The repetition of assertions and autosuggestions worked wonder. I visualized myself forgiving him, step by step, as you suggested," explained Mitali.

"Is your mind free from hatred against him?"

"Now, there is no grudge against him in my mind. There is no more revulsion of any type," said Mitali. "My mind is now free from stress, because I forgave myself also."

"Now what is your further plan?"

"I have now courage to tell him on telephone that I have forgiven him," said Mitali. "I will like to improve relations between him and my aunt. I will persuade both of them to forgive each other and come closer. I will give sincere try and I will not stop trying till, I succeed in bringing them closer to each other. I am sure, I will be successful in bringing them together again."

"You are wonderful lady. I am sure you will be successful in this noble effort also. You are a magnificent soul in a beautiful body," said Vikas. "She had rehabilitated you and it is your turn to rehabilitate her."

"Thank you very much Vikas," said Mitali with a charming smile, taking his hand in her hands. "You are so cute. You have always helped me. It will be my pleasure, if I could be of any help to you in future."

"Thank you Mitali," said Vikas. "Make it a regular practice to forgive and ask for forgiveness, as soon as possible. Be the first person to say sorry for your mistakes. I honestly believe that the simple phrases like, 'I am sorry, dear' and 'please forgive me' have done a lot to hold brothers in the home, to endear sisters to each other, to comfort mothers and fathers, to tie friends together, and to placate estranged lovers. Love of all kinds has been prompted by such phrases."

"Should we move now?" asked Vikas.

"No, not without coffee and some snacks," said Mitali pressing button of the call bell, with an alluring smile. "You have made me very happy today. I will never forget your kind gesture."

"I also had an unforgettable day with you. Thank you very much Mitali."

Chapter-13

It was a wonderful morning when Vikas woke up. Obviously, there was a bright day outside as revealed by the sunshine filtering through window fissures.

His suite was in a natural setting and it was marvelously furnished for the comfort. The windows of his room overlooked the beautiful lawn. He stood at one of the open windows and peeped outside for fresh air. Cold and fresh breeze brushed his face and he felt instantly rejuvenated. Refreshing breeze was fluttering the leaves of huge trees surrounding the area.

He felt like going out and enjoy the breeze in the lawn outside. Brilliant sunlight was inundating the verdant lawn. There were so many trees scattered in the lawn and surrounding areas, which were matted by creepers. Reena, Sofia and Shams were also walking in the lawn.

He walked through the wet velvety grass, sprinkled with dew. Bushes were replete with fragrant, bright, charming and vibrant flowers. They afforded fascination to view. The birds sang vivaciously, as if to bless the bright day.

The lawn, which was replete with seasonal flowers, looked colorful and romantic. Roses were also in full bloom, which added aroma to the air. Walking in the beautiful lawn, adorned with flowers, full of invigorating essence, refreshed him wonderfully.

"Good morning, Vikas," Reena chimed in with a charming smile. She waved at him and he waved back at her with a smile. He was walking faster and it was not easy for her to keep up with him. His stride was far longer and he seemed to move with sort of bounce of legs. He slowed down and waited for her to arrive. She came closer to Vikas galloping fast. She shook the outstretched hand and returned a smile.

"You look handsome and agile in this track suit," chirped Reena. "How was the night? You appear to be fresh and happy."

"Yes, Reena," said Vikas. "I feel fresh and energetic today. I had a wonderful sleep."

Sofia and Shams had also completed the round in the meantime and came closer.

"You all appear to be happy and joyous," remarked Vikas, looking at every body and shaking hands with all.

"Yes, we got up early and enjoyed swimming, steam bath and sauna bath together today. We had a wonderful morning," said Sofia with a charming smile. "I, generally, get up early and start my days wonderfully. Mr. Shams is also an early riser and he always gives me his company."

"Very good. We will have two sessions today. First, there will be one-to-one session with you, Shams," murmured Vikas nodding at Shams. "The second session will be in the evening. I want that Sofia should also join us."

"Okay, Vikas. It will be better," said Shams "There are a few common issues for discussion."

"Sofia, please accompany me in the evening. We will discuss the issues in the roof top restaurant with Vikas."

"Okay," cooed Sofia. "I will be ready."

Shams did his job sincerely and was a successful employee, but he, sometimes, worried a lot about his job and personal life. There had been many ups and downs in his life. Shams and Sofia had been in love with each other since the time they were studying together and they wanted to get married.

He walked up to the roof top restaurant alone enjoying the scenery in the way. He reached earlier and waited for Vikas. His countenance, as he entered the room, was joyful and contented. He sat down comfortably on the sofa and clasped his hands behind his head. Relief and an unaccountable joy filled his whole being. He was feeling comforted to think that he was getting an opportunity to release his pent up emotions and feelings.

He sauntered along to greet Vikas with a smile and shook hands.

"I hope, I did not keep you waiting," said Vikas with concern.

"No, I have just arrived," Shams apprised him with a smile.

"They also serve who stay and wait," articulated Vikas laughing. "How is life, Shams?"

"Life is wonderful," said Vikas, "and I am happy most of the time."

"Some stress and the worries which, time to time, crop up in our lives are natural," said Vikas.

"I agree, Vikas, but I, sometimes, feel overwhelmed."

"Abnormal worry is bad and we must do something about it. It is the opposite of trust and peace... It brings about nothing... It is bad for us... It diverts our attention in the wrong direction," said Vikas. "We need to get rid of this anxiety feeling."

"But how?" asked Shams.

"By analyzing the problems with a positive mental attitude... not presupposing of any problem... Thinking of solutions... playing a game... reading a book... listening to music or going to a party or movie with friends…," Vikas explained. "Did you try to get rid of worries?"

"I tried," said Shams, "but I could not succeed."

"1st analyze the problem. Find out, with a positive mental attitude, what you are worrying about. Then find out its cause. Do not be problem-oriented, but be solution-oriented," explained Vikas. "I hope you can very well do this."

"Yes."

"Okay, great," said Vikas. "Now it is time for getting solutions. Think only about solutions and note down all possible solutions. Single tasking is important. Take one problem at a time. Do it now. Analyze, as I told you and note down solutions. Have you decided which problem you are going to take up first?"

"Yes, and I have pinpointed the cause of the problem."

"Now sit comfortably and let the ideas come to your mind with an effortless ease and in free flow mode," said Vikas with a smile."

Shams gesticulated at the waiter. He came promptly and poured tea for them.

"There are a few situations, in which solution does not exist," said Shams.

"Yes, such situations will be there, but you can easily recognize them. You will know, if the problem is fixable or not. Dalai Lama had correctly expressed: '*If a problem is fixable, if a situation is such that you can do something about it, then there is no need to worry. If it's not fixable, then there is no help in worrying. There is no benefit in worrying whatsoever.*' Solution is, generally, available. You have to just find out and act on it," said Vikas.

"Very good quotation," said Shams. "I also remember a similar poem written by Mother Goose: '*For every ailment under the sun, there is a remedy, or there is none. If there be one, try to find it; if there be none, never mind it.'*

"Very good Poem, Shams. If solution is not in the sight, put the problem on a back burner to take up later or accept it," Vikas explained. "Now close your eyes and do as I told you."

"Should I tell you about the problem in detail?"

"No, there is no need. You have to deal with it," said Vikas, while relishing tea.

"I have found 5 solutions."

"Decide now, which are one or two best and most effective solutions, which will not worsen the problem," said Vikas. "After doing this, either take an effective action, or note it down to do the same later."

"I have done it."

"Okay, good. Similarly you can take up other problems, one by one."

"Sometimes, I have premonition that something bad may happen," said Shams.

"You might have realized that most of the problems we worry about never happen. We have tendency to inflate our fears," said Vikas. "Accept them as they are, with hope and faith. Once you accept the problem in its true form, your mind will be free from worries to find the solution of the problem. Even if you face such challenges, you can easily handle them. Be a tough-minded dynamic optimist and cause desired outcome to happen."

"If solution is still deluding me," said Shams. "What should I do?"

"May be, you do not have sufficient data. Wait for the data or arrange it. Till that time, put your problem on the back burner. Have patience, tomorrow is another day and sky is not going to fall."

"Thanks Vikas, I feel wonderful and relaxed now. I am sure," said Shams, "I will be able to solve the bigger problems of life in a better manner by making positive analysis and taking solution oriented action."

"I recapitulate the points to embed then into your mind to keep you happy and free from worries. Watch and share funny comedies that make you laugh… Listen to soothing, elevating music… Each day, devote some time to reading a few pages of a motivational book… Observe your thoughts… Whenever you notice negative thoughts entering your mind, switch over instantly to pleasant thoughts… Readjust your attitude and venture to change the way you look at things… Always look at the brighter aspect of life… Worries never help, but solutions do. Think, therefore, about solutions, not about worries and problems."

"Thank you very much for changing my attitude to look at the problems from a different angle."

"Always keep in mind that these are not problems but challenges. If you face these challenges with a positive mental attitude, you will emerge stronger to face bigger challenges of life. Be bold to take bull by horn. God has given you sufficient strength to face them boldly and prosper. An abundant life is waiting for you," said Vikas with empathy. "See you in the evening with Sofia."

Shams was contented and joyful after meeting Vikas. He looked forward to meet him again in the evening with Sofia. He picked up a magazine and flipped through it, till he felt sleepy. He did not know when he slept. He got up fresh and relaxed. He was ready to move when he heard a rap on his door. Sofia entered the room with a charming smile. She looked fresh and beautiful.

"Are you ready?" asked Sofia. "Should we move?"

"Yes, darling. I was waiting for you," mumbled Shams. He stood up and hugged her.

It was a pleasant walk in the thick lush green forest. Sofia and Shams were enraptured with its scenic beauty. They had often come together earlier for a walk in this forest and had a wonderful time together. Today also they decided to walk to the tree top restaurant together. They had so many pleasant memories related to the forest. They both loved nature and posting at this resort, which they had anyhow managed to get, gave them ample time to explore pristine nature.

He took her hand, and they came under a huge tree, with a potent wealth of branches. Creepers, full of brilliant flowers had encircled branches, which looked wonderful. Bushes replete with colorful fragrant flowers, surrounded the lower trunk and roots.

They sat down on an elevated root. The air amazingly flawless, assuaging, fragrant and sweet with the purity of the forest. For some time, they were enchanted and speechless. There was no perceptible sound except that of the breeze, the buzz of the bees, and the chirping of the birds in the branches. The birds whistled and sang the songs softly to their brooding mates in the thick hedges.

Shams pulled Sofia closer in his arms and raised her chin. He kissed her cheeks and forehead. Noticing his enhanced heart beats, she squirmed in his arms and hid her face in his chest. He noticed that his own heart beats were synchronizing with her enhanced heartbeats.

She was so intensely conscious that words stumbled and were lame. She could manage only a few syllables at a time. Both kept quiet for some time and looked at each other with love. An inexpressible peace swept like the breath of heaven through the aromatic flowers. They sat down sighing for bliss. The silence became too eloquent. She drew in a deep breath, moistening her lips with the tip of her tongue, unable to figure out what she wanted to say, but she felt that she wanted to say something to break the silence.

"Do not do that," groaned Shams.

"Do what?" she mumbled, confused.

"This," he demonstrated angling his head, so as to replace the moistness of her tongue on her lips with his own. His tongue swept across her lips arousingly.

"Naughty and insatiable boy," said Sofia, responding with a tight seductive hug and a deep kiss.

"You, probably, do not know, how tempted I have always been to taste you just this way," he said smiling and trying to control his breath.

"Do not act silly," said Sofia with a naughty smile. "You are unquenchable... As if you are doing it for the first time."

"Should we move, Sofia? Vikas might have come."

"Yes honey, let us go."

For a few minutes they kept sauntering along the delightful path, till a sudden turn brought them sight of the exquisite tree top restaurant, surrounded by huge trees.

Vikas had already reached there and there was nobody else except him and a waiter. He welcomed Sofia and Shams with a bright smile. They all sat on sofa chairs around the round center table. It was always a pleasing experience to sit and talk in such an exotic and natural environment. Cold breeze, filtering through leaves, plants and bushes mingled with the natural aroma of the forest and provided olfactory delight. Flower plants were well looked after and were replete with brilliant flowers.

"How is the day?" asked Vikas smiling charmingly, looking at each of them, one by one.

"The day is wonderful," said Sofia with a smile.

Shams nodded at waiter to bring tea and coffee.

"Sir, what will you like to have tea or coffee?" asked waiter.

"Coffee," said Vikas.

"We all will take coffee," added Sofia, "with some snacks."

"How is your love life, Sofia?" Vikas blurted out coming straight to the point without any preliminaries.

"Wonderful," said Sofia, shame facedly, handing over cup of coffee to Vikas and Shams with a smile. "We had magnificent time together. There are, however, a few problems from our family members and relatives. They are against our marriage."

"What is reason?" asked Vikas.

"Social and religious," said Sofia. "They are vehemently opposed to our marriage. They think that differences in lifestyle of both the communities will adversely affect our happiness and future relationship."

"There is no doubt that your parents want to see you happy. They are thinking for your welfare. You both have to persuade your parents that you both will be happy together and you can easily adjust in the changed scenario and social environment. Once they are convinced that time has changed a lot and such marriages are becoming common these days, they will no more object to your conjugal relationship," Vikas assured them convincingly. "Do not forget that your choice and happiness is more important than anything else. Osho used to say: '*Get out of your head and get into your heart. Think less, feel more.*' Are you a Hindu, by religion?"

"No, Vikas. I am a Christian," Sofia uttered. "We have absolutely no religious prejudices. We respect each other's religions and all religions as they are," said Sofia in a calm, well-bred manner and Shams nodded in approval, which amused Vikas.

"I am a Muslim," Shams interjected after a pause.

"How passionately do you both desire to get married to each other? How do you like 'live in' relationship? It is now legal. It is a significant way to explore compatibility." Vikas muttered. "When are you going to get married?"

"We actually do not believe in 'live in' relationship, this is why we always lived separately within norms, in different houses. We have decided to get married very soon," said Shams. "I have, however, not yet decided about the date. We have to first persuade our parents to bless us."

"If they do not agree, then what should we do?" asked Sofia.

"You tell me which options do you have to choose from?"

"In that situation, I think, the court marriage is the only option available to us," said Shams. "I have, however, decided it as the last option."

"In that case also, you should be constantly in contact with your parents and keep talking with them. Communicate often with each other's parents also. Try to be as friendly as possible. Do not be dissuaded by the resistance. You may take help of a few other relatives also to persuade them. Do you have such relatives?"

"Yes, my maternal uncle and one of my father's friend are very helpful," chimed in Sofia. "I have requested them and they are doing their best to persuade them. They are successful to some extent."

"Very good. Goals should be specific with specific date. I am sure you will persuade them with your consistent efforts," said Vikas, standing to move on the other side of the restaurant. "Decide now in consultation with each other, the additional steps you are going to take to persuade them and specific period and date for marriage."

Vikas continued walking in balcony, till the discussion continued between Sofia and Shams. Vikas came back on his seat after 10 minutes and raised his glance at them. They appeared contented and relieved.

"We have decided the specific date for marriage and also explored some more ways to persuade our parents. We are hopeful for positive results," said Sofia. "I feel now free and relieved."

"Thank you very much Vikas for giving us time to help us find solution to the challenge, we are facing," said Sofia. "Thanks for encouragement and motivation."

"Thank you Vikas for relieving my mind and making it free from stress," said Shams. "I will be glad, if I can be of any help in future."

"Do not forget to invite me for the party," said Vikas, laughing with hilarity.

"We will certainly invite you, Vikas," cooed Sofia with her usual smile.

Chapter-14

Reena was extremely happy today. She was all the time thinking about Vikas. Sweet memories of wonderful moments spent with him still lingered in her mind. She was again eager to go for the date with him. She always felt immensely comfortable and blissful in his company. She was charmed by his personality and wanted to come closer to him.

"Do I have crush on him? Do I love him? Or is it temporary feeling? Does he have any such feeling for me? Do I want dates with him, interspersed with flowers and kisses?" she asked herself so many questions.

"Whatever may be answer of these questions, I am going to make the most of his company and have a wonderful time with him," she mused.

She was happy that Vikas had promised to meet her in the evening.

Vikas got fresh and decided to take tea before going out. There was a gentle rap on the door and Reena entered smiling.

"I hope you are ready, Vikas."

"Yes, dear. Please sit down," said Vikas with a smile. "Let us, first, take tea, before we go out."

"Okay."

There was another soft rap on the door and waiter entered the room. He poured tea for them and went out.

"Thank you very much for sparing time from your busy schedule," said Reena with a charming smile. "Every moment I spent so far with you have been delightful. I always relish your company."

"I also like your company, Reena," said Vikas. "You are a sweet, young and charming lady."

"Where are we going for a walk?" asked Reena, sipping tea and looking fondly at him.

"I think, the nearby park in the forest is a better option. It is only at a walking distance. What do you think? Please let me know, if you have a better spot to suggest."

"I like your choice," said Reena, "That is a wonderful place to visit. I had been there once, with Mitali. It is a marvelous place to visit."

It was a beautiful weather. The blazing heat had, by now, subsided to a considerable extent and breeze was quite soothing. The departing sun peeped from the drifting cloudlets. The air was abounding with the fragrance of lilac, lavender and wild cherry. Chirping of birds blended with the rustle of leaves created enchanting music.

"Walking with you in this beautiful ambience is a delightful experience," said Reena.

"I also like to spend time with you here. You are so magnificent and dazzling. I always feel happy in your company and like to share a few beautiful moments with you. Who will not like to enjoy company of such a beautiful and glamorous lady?" said Vikas appreciatingly. "I am charmed by your jest for living and cheerful attitude."

"You are a magnificent person to hang out with. I never felt as happy as I am, whenever I am with you."

"It will always be my pleasure, if I could put a smile on your flowery face," chimed in Vikas.

"Thanks, Vikas."

"Do not you have close friends?" asked Vikas. "You are a successful and glamorous lady. There may be so many persons who would like to do anything to win your heart and be your friend."

"True; there are people galore who are after glamour. They desire to come closer and want to be my friends. But I did not find someone with whom I may develop close friendship and deeper bond. They are all just acquaintances."

"Try to explore; there may be a few who are sincere," said Vikas. "Did you try dating any of them?"

"Yes, a few times," said Reena, "but I did not get a good lasting companion."

"You are a successful young lady and you have so many qualities. When time is ripe, somebody will recognize these qualities and reach out to you with an intent of a meaningful relationship," said Vinod encouragingly. "I am surprised you have not got any good friend so far."

"To be frank, I had a strange feelings when I met you first."

"Wow, I am happy you have such feelings for me," Vinod chuckled, putting his hand on her shoulder and looking deep into her eyes. "I also like you very much and feel very happy with you."

"Do you have such feelings for me?" asked Reena hesitatingly. "I mean, do you have a crush on me?"

"It is too early to say. I have never thought on these lines." said Vikas ruminating. "You are a magnificent friend; there is no doubt about it. I assure you, I will always be your friend, a lasting and a longtime friend. I always feel happy with you."

"Thanks, it is enough for me," she said hugging him. He responded with a warm compassionate hug.

Chapter-15

Meena was a bit tired and needed some rest. She took shower and slipped into bath tub. After taking bath she was feeling relaxed but still somnolent. She took out a book on relaxing meditation to relax in the bed. She did not remember when she slept, but woke up fresh and joyful. She decided to start her day wonderfully. She opened window and what she saw lifted her spirits. There was a slight trace of mist and the breeze was soothing. Bushes in the lawn were full of bright and colorful flowers. She looked outside, resting on her elbows and practiced deep breathing for some time. She went out to take a few rounds in the lawn. She instantly felt rejuvenated and joyful.

She took steam and sauna bath together with Reena and Mitali. She did swimming and frolicked around in the pool with Reena and Mitali, till she was totally exhausted. She came back to her room and changed the dress for breakfast. Comfortably ensconced on sofa, she closed her eyes for deep breathing and relaxed for a few minutes. She opened her eyes when she heard a gentle rap on door.

"Please come in," said Meena.

"Good morning, Dr. Meena," Vinod squeaked, stepping inside the room with his ebullient smile. "You are looking alive, active and fresh, Meena. Are you ready for the breakfast?"

"Thanks Vinod, please come. I was thinking about you." cooed Meena with jubilation, as if she was waiting for him. She looked at him with her heart tumbling over with love. She got up, sauntered along toward him, hugged him and ruffled his hairs affectionately. His heart rate quickened to notice her joy and love for him. She sat on the side, creating space for him on the sofa.

"We have ample time. We may go for breakfast after 20 minutes or so. We will sit together and talk here for some time. I missed you a lot," mumbled Meena with a butter-soft voice, looking into his eyes with love.

"Really? I have also been thinking about you," said Vinod. "You did not tell me about your passion, Meena," said Vinod after a brief pause, settling comfortably on sofa beside her.

"I passionately wanted to become a doctor," said Meena. "I am grateful to God for blessing me with my cherished desire."

"This is a wonderful achievement. Nowadays competitions are very tough. You have to work smart," said Vinod.

"What do you mean by working smart?"

"Here 'smart' means: 1. S--*specific*. For example, "I will lose 10 pounds in 90 days. M--must be *measurable* so that you can monitor progress. A--must be *achievable*, otherwise it will becomes creepy. R--*Realistic*; to lose 50 pounds in 30 days is unrealistic. T--*Time-bound*; there should be a starting and a finishing."

"Okay, thanks for explaining, Vinod," said Meena. "I required lot of money for that. I have a firm belief that, if you are passionate enough and work incessantly for you cherished desire, the universe arranges to deliver it to you somehow. My family members did all they could to provide needed help. I am happy and grateful to God that I achieved my coveted goal and became a doctor."

"This is a grand achievement indeed," said Vinod appreciating. "We always attract what we wish fervently and think about with passion and strong desire."

"Yes darling. Now I believe, what you pay attention on grows and expands. If you resolutely follow your passion, you will always get it. If you are grateful to God, all the blockages are removed. You get what you require, whether it is money or other goals," said Meena. "Law of attraction always works and you always get what you are passionate about."

"What is your next target?"

"I want to open my own clinic, where I can serve people, and at the same time, earn money to live a comfortable life, without becoming a burden on my 'would be' husband," said Dr. Meena. "Tell me about you. I am eager to know more about you, dear."

"You will be surprised to know that my father also wanted to have his own clinic. Accordingly, he arranged to get one of his own. He appointed a few Doctors to run it. Later my sister also became a doctor and she efficiently handled it. I wished that she continued to look after it, but she got married to a doctor in Australia and she moved there. She advised me to get a doctor wife to look after it," Vinod muttered with an enigmatic smile, which was more eloquent than his words.

"Wow, your sister is also a doctor!" exclaimed Meena. "I will like to meet her someday."

"She will also be glad to meet you, I am sure," said Vinod with his usual smile.

"Who is that lucky girl who is going to look after that clinic and you? Did you meet her? I will like to meet her too."

"I think I have met her," said Vinod with a mysterious smile. "But I have not yet proposed her to marry me."

"Does she know that you have a crush on her?" asked Meena inquisitively, her eyes lit up with curiosity. "Did you tell her that you love her? Does she also love you?"

"I think so," said Vinod. "Though she has not yet communicated her feelings."

"You are still in the 'I think so' stage. It is very bad. Why have you not proposed to her, yet? You should have taken an initiative to probe her," Meena pontificated with a concern. "Had you been bold enough to propose marriage to her, probably, you might have been married to her by now."

"I would feel too much hurt, if she refused," Vinod murmured with a smile. "Her refusal might have devastated me."

"Come on. Be a man, take a chance and assert yourself for your own sake. Fear of refusal should not deter you from accomplishing your passionate desires. You have all qualifications to be a magnificent husband," Meena reassured him encouragingly. "Propose marriage to her at the earliest, may be even just now on phone, if you are not able to meet her soon."

"Okay, I will let you know her response. I will talk to her."

"Why do not you call her now?" she prompted him.

"Okay," he mumbled. He took out the mobile phone and searched a number to call. In the meantime, there was a ring on her telephone.

"Vinod, please wait a minute," said Dr. Meena, turning back and moving aside in the corner of the room.

"Hi, darling. I love you my sweetheart. I would be honored to marry a gorgeous young lady like you. Do I stand a chance?"

Dr. Meena was struck dumb with an amazement to recognize the voice of Vinod and whirled around furiously to teach him a lesson. But it was too late. He clasped her from behind and kissed her neck.

"Vinod, it is not a good joke," she yelled with false annoyance. She was still confused. She tried to free herself, squirming in her tight arms.

First, Vinod was a bit confused, then he regained his composure and said with a deep sigh, "I think, I have really messed things up. I should have, better, asked you first, not told you. I think I should not have opened my mind. Can you pretend you did not hear what I uttered, sweetie?"

"Sorry dear, I thought you are joking," said Meena.

"It is not a joke, sweetie… I am not joking… I am serious and…," affirmed Vinod, looking into her eyes, "I love you my sweetheart."

There were pauses in the conversation, as if the ideas called up were only elusive straws floating in the air. Then a hot passion of tenderness filled their hearts. For a long time she nestled to him, and he kissed her softly; her hairs, her face, her forehead, her eye lids, her ears, gently and softly. They looked into each other's eyes for a long time.

She was in a dreamy state, until his warm breath on her ears concerned her again, kindling her fires. His physical fascination was hypnotic. She had to try hard to resist its influence and regain her composure. Very gently he put an arm around her, and lifted her chin with a tender delicacy of touch. They hugged each other passionately for a long time.

She eased herself gently from his clasp. She silently withdrew to a corner of the room and then sauntered slowly, a few times forward and backward and then toward the half open window, seeming to watch the trees out of the window bars with a grim face. Mild moonlight filtering through bars was falling on her calm face. He moved towards her with a slow pace and clasped her with both of his hands, looking into her streaming eyes. He noticed that her face was changing colors. He wiped her eyes and kissed her forehead softly.

"Say you love me, darling. Say 'I love you' to me," Vinod pleaded desperately. "I am eager to hear these words from you, sweetie."

He put his arms around her again. This time she also put her hands on his shoulder, looking down at him with strange lighted eyes, very tender, but with a curious look lurking underneath.

What a joy! What a hallucination of bliss! Her heart was a pure blaze. She was purely comatose in elation. She moved closer towards him and clang to him in sheer ecstasy. Both remained still and unconscious under the spell of the magical charm. Then she mumbled with a butter-soft voice, "I also love you, Vinod."

"I am so ecstatic to hear these sweet words. Thank you very much Meena," said Vinod joyously and hugged her again.

The antique clock on wall asseverated with ten distinct strokes reminding them that they were getting late for the breakfast.

"We are getting late, Vinod," said Dr. Meena. "Let us go and have the breakfast."

"Okay," said Vinod. "Can we go for an evening walk today?"

"Why not? I also wanted to say the same thing. Thank you, Vinod," said Dr. Meena with elation.

"I will pick you up in the evening."

~~~

All were already present in the hall when the 'just became' couple entered the dining hall. They had already started taking the breakfast when Vinod and Dr Meena reached in the dining hall. Their entry made a sensation, as all the glances were raised towards them. John and Mitali whispered with an enigmatic smile looking at them. Shams and Reena rose and galloped ahead to welcome them. Others just smiled and lifted their glances, lit up with curiosity. They noticed that the dining room was sensitive and lively. The hall was flooded with a soft light; it was full of the perfume of flowers. The color of silken curtains was brilliant. The aroma of delectable food, the tinkle of crystals on the chandelier, the low murmur of happy voices, the occasional thrill of sudden laughter, and the delicious accompaniment of soft, sensuous music completed the charm of the room. It was impossible to resist its influence.

"Welcome, Dr. Meena and Vinod," squeaked Sofia with a joyous voice. "We have been waiting for you both."

"Thank you very much," said Vinod acknowledging the welcome.

"Where have you been?" Mitali asked with an inquisitive voice and a charming smile.

"Thank you friends, for the concern," said Meena. "Actually, Vinod came to my room. We had to discuss some important issues."

"We are planning for a joint venture," said Vinod with an uneasy smile. Vinod blushed perfectly crimson during this explanation, as if he had come with the most improper excuse.

"Really?" said Mitali looking at both with an enigmatic smile. "You must take our addresses and please make sure that you do not forget to invite us in the reception party of your joint venture."

"What can I say? These are your own musings. You can illustrate situations in your own way," said Meena with a bright smile.

Then something amazing happened. All nodded at each other. The whole group stood up and came together making a ring around them and showered them with heartfelt blessings... leaving them flabbergasted. They felt very happy about the act regarding a new life they were keen to start together.

Everybody appeared in an amusing and joyful mood. Vinod was over joyous today. Meena was also ecstatic. She enjoyed all the humorous, entertaining things he said. The breakfast became more delicious and interesting by his fine hilarity, pleasant anecdotes and amusing remarks.

~~~

He was ready when Dr. Meena came and knocked at his door. He opened the door, as if he was already waiting for her eagerly. As soon as she entered in the room, he closed the door. He turned and gathered her in his arms. She raised her eyes gradually, with a sizzling, penetrating and flaming look into his eyes. His psyche was filled with her blazing recognition. This time she did not hesitate to respond with a tighter hug.

"Should we go now for a walk?"

"Yes, I am ready."

"I think we should go out with an umbrella that too to some nearby place, as the possibility of rains cannot be ruled out."

"Meena, you are correct. It may rain any time."

It was an exquisite experience to walk in the forest in this weather. The cold breeze, impregnated with rain droplets was brushing their cheeks.

There was lightning followed by thunder. Speed of the wind had also increased by now.

"There is a possibility of thunder storm and heavy rains," said Meena, noticing continuous flash. Vinod took out a hanky and wiped her face, raising her chin. She hugged him tight and rested her head on his chest. He took her in his arms and drew her closer to his chest to keep her warm.

They realized that the storm, which had, for some time, been brewing, was becoming more ferocious. Time to time, dazzling flash of lightning inundated the trees and grass lands. As they walked, sudden flash of lightning cut through the sky, followed almost instantaneously by a long, growl of thunder. The drops of rain began to fall. Time to time, thunder cracked and lightening flashed and the dazzling flash light was immediately followed by a thunder. They had hardly traversed some distance when they perceived more frequent lightening in the sky. It was a joyful sight, for it was harbinger of heavy rain. Now the boisterous wind had started roaring among the trees and bushes.

"How do you like the experience?" asked Vinod walking joyfully.

"It is a wonderful experience to walk with an adventurous man, like you, even in this ferocious weather."

His arm was around her waist, her head was almost on his shoulder, and both were thrilled. Cold wind knifed through her dress.

They were visualizing refreshing precipitation. Within an instant, they were drenched with water. They stopped under a tree. He looked at her fondly, with lucid and blissful eyes. His face glowed with a certain radiant pleasure. He was very happy today with her. She looked down at him, captivated, so deeply connected in fascinated magnetism.

He looked into her eyes. Beauty of her eyes was filled with abnormal brilliance. They sat in stillness on a rock under the tree for some time and then walked in the open area to enjoy the blissful drizzle. She shivered, as cold breeze brushed her wet torso and face. He pulled her closer and wiped her face with his hand. She received the heavenly communication in his touches. She heard all she wanted to hear and felt all she wanted to feel by the slightest touch of his hand, as his touches were more eloquent than words. She reciprocated by hugging him tight. Even in the darkness of the cloudy evening, her beauty shone with the brilliance of a bright flower among the foliage.

"How wonderful to walk like this in the forest in such a stormy weather!" she exclaimed, smiling at him in the most ravishing way. She gave him a comprehensively admiring glance.

"Let us go back now," Meena suggested. She gave her unusual little uplift of the head, which was one of her many captivating gestures. "We must go back now and change."

"Like to have coffee?" asked Vinod, reaching his suite.

"Yes, darling," said Meena. "I will be back soon after taking a shower in my suite," assured Meena, looking at her wet dress and then looking at him, who was already looking at her fondly with furtive glances.

"Okay honey, I will wait for you after getting fresh. Thanks for your company. I will always relish the memory of these wonderful moments, I have shared with you today."

Hearing a gentle knock, he opened the door for her and settled on sofa. His face appeared flushed and pinkish.

"Vinod, what is this? Are you okay?"

He did not speak. He tried to hide his anguish with a feeble smile. She touched his neck with her fingers fearing fever.

"Oh my God! You have fever," she mumbled with concern. "You are not well, Vinod. You require a bed rest. I will bring some medicine for you in a jiffy," said Dr. Meena, examining him thoroughly. She galloped out to fetch medicines from her suite. She returned with medicines and placed order for coffee. Waiter came with coffee and poured it for them. He took medicine and felt immense relief after taking coffee with her.

"Please sit comfortably or lie down on bed," she admonished, adjusting his posture and brushing his hairs softly with her fingers. "You will be okay soon. I am sorry to have cast my shadow over your evening. I should not have insisted for an outing in such an inclement weather."

"Do not be silly, my sweetheart. It is not your fault. I wanted to go out with you. It was I, who insisted to go out in this weather. Take it easy. I am feeling quite comfortable now, sitting with you," Vinod mumbled in his usual simple and calm voice nestling his head on her shoulder. He seemed so calmly and sanely candid that she moved a bit on the side and helped him put and rest his head on her lap. Feeling, comfortable, he closed his eyes and took a short nap.

After relaxing nap, he opened his eyes, hearing her soft voice.

"I hope you are relaxed now."

"Yes, to a considerable extent," said Vinod with a mild smile, determinedly. "I feel immensely comfortable now, after relaxing nap."

"Okay, I will let you feel even better," said Meena with an enigmatic smile. "Please sit straight, head resting on the back of sofa... close your eyes... Take deep breath...

tense every part of body while inhaling... release them while exhaling... relax your face and ease the grimace... relax your forehead... relax and half open your lips... and take breath through your mouth... Imagine a crimson rose touching your lips and you smell its fragrance..."

He was jolted out of dreamy state when he felt warm breath approaching nearer. Before he came to his sense, her pair of lips touched his lips. He experienced her tight hug and wild heart beats synchronizing with his. It was not a platonic kiss upon the forehead, not a brotherly kiss upon the cheek, but a fervent and passionate kiss upon the slightly parted lips, a kiss of worship and amazement... It was a kiss, like the one, with which Adam, in all probability, had awakened Eve. Her kiss was passionate, persistent and demanding and he reciprocated that demand with his own. He was shaken and stunned and transported to a different world. They kissed for a long time, till their mild fire reached forest fire proportions.

He opened his eyes, but he felt that he was still a bit dreamy. She looked at him avidly. The storm had passed. He was now quieter in her arms. The sweet wine of love entered his brain like heavenly nectar. He was floating in the sky on the cloud nine. Grateful smile emerged and flickered on his lips. The surprise was so inordinate; it rendered him flabbergasted, stunned and speechless.

"How do you feel now, honey?" Meena quipped with a smile. "Now you take rest on the bed and take another nap. I will come after some time."

"I feel that I am floating in the sky. Today I realized that the first kiss is the most exquisite cloudburst moment in life, especially when you least expect it," he explained whispering softly. "May I ask you something?"

"Yes."

"Will you marry me?"

She was flabbergasted to hear the words for a few moments. There was a stunned silence for some time. Her internal dialogues were reduced to a few polysyllabic questions. She pondered for a while and wanted to say, *"It is above belief... I cannot believe... it is beyond belief... Are you proposing a lifetime of togetherness? ... Are you making up a story to tease me?"*

Blushing profusely, she struggled to regain her balance and semblance of composure. She groped for suitable words in vain and could only murmur, "I have already told you that I love you darling," said Meena.

"That I know honey," said Vinod. "But this time I am proposing marriage. If you take the risk of marrying me, I assure you, you will never regret doing so."

"Who am I to say 'no' in that case?" Meena giggled with an enchanting smile. "I will be glad to marry you. I love you, my sweetheart," Meena reassured him, flinging her arms around his neck. He felt her warm breath on his neck.

"Why do you want to marry me?"

"Because you are a wonderful and a caring lady, an amazing lover. You are also going to be an exceptional mother of our children."

"But why do you want children?" she poked him joyfully, with enigmatic smile.

"Because we cannot have grandchildren, if we do not have children," Vinod whispered with a butter-soft voice, as his grip tightened and his mouth came down to hers. He kissed her again, passionately and thoroughly.

"Be here now in this moment," said Dr. Meena, laughing. "Make your dwelling place in the present moment, my dear. Live in the day-tight compartment up to bed time."

"But visiting future for planning is not a bad idea, darling," said Vikas laughing, "provided you have your dwelling place in the present moment."

She was extremely happy in his arms. Her heart swelled with pride. She mused, "*I am so joyful to be proposed by a person who is so caring and so lovely. He has sense of humor and zest for living. He is masculine, adventurous and daring. He dresses well and behaves courteously. The loveliness of his disposition is enchanting. He is well settled and financially independent. He welcomes and hugs so gracefully. His arm are so strong to feel around. His eyes are full of tenderness. What else I need. Thank you God for your wonderful gift.*"

Chapter-16

John was very happy today. He was happy that he came here to attend the workshop at this beautiful resort. He had a magnificent time in this resort. It was a wonderful change from a dull mundane routine. He realized that there was a positive change in his attitude towards life. He was still, time to time, feeling dejected and disconsolate. He tried to find out the cause, but could not do so. This workshop gave him an ample opportunity to re-examine his attitude towards his life. His attitude was slowly changing from negative to positive.

He was, nowadays feeling on the top of the hill and the reason for his euphoria was his friendship with Mitali. He had been feeling extremely happy, since he went for a few outings with her. He, first time, had realized that life was more wonderful than he had ever imagined.

He wanted to formally propose to Mitali, but he realized that time was not yet ripe, as all was not well with her. She was taking time to reveal her deep routed melancholy. She had promised to meet him that day and discuss everything frankly. She was waiting for counseling from Vikas who had met her yesterday in a one-to-one session.

He still felt, time to time, that something was missing in his own life as well. He decided to take an effective remedial action. He had discussed earlier his problem with Vikas. Vikas assured him to help him find out the deep routed cause for his problem. Both decided to meet in the evening and discuss in detail.

Most of the time he was thinking about Mitali. He relished the memory of every moment spent with her. She was the most glamorous and the most beautiful lady who came in his life and became so close to him in such a short time.

Mitali reached his suit, rang the bell and waited. She was willing to wait until the door opened. John was taking tea on his bed when he heard a gentle rap on the door. On opening the door, he found Mitali standing in front of him, beaming with delight. She was in a cream color track suit and looked charming.

"Good morning!" said Mitali with enticing smile, as she entered the room. Her face was radiant with a delightful smile. Both hugged each other.

"You appear to be fresh and joyful darling," John squeaked. "I have never seen you so happy earlier."

"Yes darling, I am on the cloud nine."

"I can figure out the reason," John mumbled with a smile. "How was the meeting with Vikas?"

"Superb," Mitali chuckled with a seductive smile. "It could not be better. I feel free and relieved."

"Relieved? What happened? Tell me in detail." John prompted her with an insatiable intrinsic curiosity.

"Not now, sweetie. We will go out for a short walk in the park," Mitali chuckled with a seductive smile.

"Will you like to have tea?"

"No thanks, I have already taken," said Mitali standing up.

John also stood up along with her. He wrapped his arms around her shoulders and hugged her tightly, before she could turn around to move.

"I invited you for a walk, not for a hug," she mumbled with a naughty smile, responding his hug. "Okay darling, let us go. We will not go far away, so that we can return well before breakfast."

"Okay, darling," said John. "Could you forgive him?"

"Yes completely," said Mitali with a sigh of relief. "There is no more resentment against him in my mind. Later I talked to him on phone. It was a pleasant surprise for him."

"Was he really sorry for what he had done to you?" asked John with curious concern.

"Yes. He had said sorry earlier also, but this time he was extremely happy that I telephoned him and I have accepted his apology," said Mitali with a peaceful demeanor. "Now I am going to take an initiative to improve relations between him and aunty."

"Can we sit down for some time?" asked Mitali. "I feel exhausted."

"Yes, why not darling," said John. "Let us sit down for some time and relax."

He sat down on the grass and Mitali placed his head in his lap.

"You are sweating, sweetie," said John looking into her eyes and combing her hairs with his fingers. He took out a hanky and wiped her forehead. He held her shoulders with his both hands and raised her nearer to him. She did not resist him this time. Her eyes were closed and lips relaxed and half parted. First of all, he softly kissed her eyes and then her lips. She hugged him clasping his neck, putting her hands behind the neck, resting her hands on his nape and responded with hot marathon kisses.

"You did not tell me what you are going to discuss with Vikas today in one-to-one session?" asked Mitali with an intrinsic curiosity.

"I will let you know after I discuss with him today," responded John. "It is mainly related to my business, happiness and satisfaction with my life."

"Okay dear."

~~~~~~~

Vikas was already ensconced in a comfortable cane-chair when John reached poolside lawn.

"Hi, good morning Vikas," squeaked John with a smile.

"Good morning, John." Vikas responded with a smile. "Are you happy?"

"I am very happy nowadays. I am generally happy," said John, "but only occasionally I feel despondent."

"Please sit down and make yourself comfortable…" murmured Vikas, pointing towards a chair in front of him. "How is your business?"

"I inherited a well settled business, a steel industry and a big fortune from my father."

"Are you satisfied with your business?" asked Vikas. "Do you get real satisfaction from your business?"

"Not exactly. I find something missing," articulated John after a pause. "I am earning a lot. I run a big business and there are so many employees. My business is quite stable and there is no need to put some extra effort. I do not require more money."

"Stable? Feeling comfortable? Not growing? Is there a targeted growth? No need for an extra effort?" asked Vikas.

John was groping for words to reply so many question. He seemed to re-examine the questions silently.

"Take your own time to find the honest answers." Vikas prompted him.

"I have not paid much attention to these points," said John. "I believed that I have already got enough and extra money would create more problems."

"This attitude is creating the problems. Money is a very good thing, whether it is with you or with someone else. Never be jealous of others abundance. Earn it and help others to earn it. Spend it wisely and invest it to grow. You have to be richer," advised Vikas. "Invest more, take more risks. Let the wealth and abundance grow by leap and bounds. While doing all this, do not neglect the growth."

"I never thought on these lines earlier, Vikas," said John. "Thank you for inspiring me to look at the things from a different angle."

"Abundance does not create problems, but it solves the problems," explained Vikas. "Your problem is that you feel that you are successful and you feel that there is no need to grow and you have all you want."

"Do not you think that feeling of abundance is a good thing?" asked John.

"Yes, you are correct," replied Vikas. "Feeling of abundance gives you immense contentment. It gives freedom to develop your creativity. It relieves you from fear of poverty, which is a stumbling block in way of success and joy for many," said Vikas. "You must enjoy your abundance without feeling guilty and you must be grateful to God for his blessings. But at the same time, you must work smarter and harder to grow, to let the abundance increase."

"Okay," said John. "It is a wonderful advice."

"Having abundance is not enough. Growth is even more important. You have to grow and move ahead. Grow and have more abundance, if you want to get real satisfaction," said Vikas. "Constantly work smart for self-growth and growth of your business. Invest in research and sharpening the tools.

There is enough room for improvement in every field. John Wooden used to say: '*When you improve a little each day, eventually big things occur. When you improve conditioning a little each day, eventually you have a big improvement in conditioning. Not tomorrow, not the next day, but eventually a big gain is made. Don't look for the big, quick improvement. Seek the small improvement one day at a time. That's the only way it happens -- and when it happens, it lasts.*' There is more than enough in this world for everybody."

"What steps should I take to constantly grow and improve?" asked John inquisitively.

"Set a target for growth. Prosper and earn more money. You have yet to reach the pinnacle. You will be able to help more persons and spend more in charity. You can open new branches to give more employment to needy persons," Vikas elaborated. "Prepare a passion card and get busy achieving your passion."

"What is a passion card?" asked John with curiosity. "How can I prepare it?"

"We will discuss it in detail," said Vikas. "First let us have coffee with some snacks."

Waiter placed the tray down and poured the coffee in the cups.

It was partially a cloudy day and there were a few small patches of clouds in the sky. Cold breeze was brushing their cheeks. It was a pleasant experience to sit in the lawn near pool.

"Please be more comfortable... Now, close your eyes and practice relaxed breathing... as I explained earlier... Relax every part of your body... one by one... Recognize 5 different sounds you hear..." expatiated Vikas in detail. "Now observe, if there is any tension in any part of your body… Stretch that part and relax while exhaling. Now think about your 10 passions."

"Can you explain further how I can do it?" asked John.

"You already know what you are passionate about," said Vikas looking into his eyes. "Asking yourself following questions, before writing down your 10 passions, will be helpful: *'What is my vision of future, mission and chief aim?'…'What is my passion and ambition and what I want to become, get and do?'…'Where will I like to be after 1 year, two years, five years and 10 years from now?'…'How I want to be remembered after my death?'…'what is important to me; is it advancement of career or love of family or achieving success a top priority?'* Honest answers of these questions will be helpful."

"I have written down 10 of my passions, as you suggested," said John after a pause.

"Okay, well done," said Vikas. "Now, your list is ready; compare 1st desire with the remaining 9 in the list, one-by-one. Tick the item which you desire most. Then again take up 2nd and compare with the remaining items except the one already chosen."

"If the second is already ticked/chosen?" asked John.

"Then take the 1st and compare with remaining."

"Thus decide the 2nd desire. Now take up the third, unticked in the list and compare with the remaining 7 unticked desires. Continue, till you decide 5 top desires. Now, note down these 5 desires on a blank card. This is your passion card. Keep it with you and refer to it time to time, till your subconscious takes over," said Vikas. "Do it now as I told you. I will help you."

"Okay."

"Whenever you brainstorm, prepare the comprehensive list and prioritize things to do, daily or weekly, make sure, your list is in conformity with your passion card."

"Be contented, but not self-righteously complacent, so as to become lethargic. Lack of mental stimulation tends to induce tedium and dullness. Things are always very exciting when your brain has a challenge and is constructively and creatively occupied," explained Vikas. "You must also set a goal. The goals, which you set for yourself, always inspire you to continue going ahead in life."

"Now, I can figure out, where I went wrong. Thanks for explaining in detail," said John. "I will work harder, with more enthusiasm to find out my passions and achieve them."

"Smarter, not harder… You should enjoy life… Once you complete a task successfully, have a little break without feeling guilty and enjoy leisure. You always deserve relaxation, break and gratification," said Vikas. "Before going to bed, analyze with a positive mental attitude, how exactly you spent your day and also what you have to do the next day."

"Fantastic suggestion," said John.

"You should always keep your vision, chief aim and your mission in your mind. If you want to make continuous improvements in your performance and continually push your limits, it is important that you set goals for yourself and follow through on a plan to accomplish them," Vikas reiterated. "You should never sit idle, thinking that you already have enough."

"Okay."

"You should always have a feeling of abundance and you should express your gratitude to God for it," explained Vikas, "but it should encourage you for more energetic and enthusiastic actions. This feeling should motivate you to set higher limits and achieve them. Stop worrying about things that may or may not happen and start being thankful for the things you have right now. Developing an attitude of gratitude can transform our state of mind. Spend a few minutes each day, listing things for which you are thankful."

"Now I realize that there is no time to sit idle," said John with smile. "Now the target is clear. I will now be able to make prompt decisions on what more requires to be done. I am grateful to God for inheriting abundance and I am going to work harder and smarter to make it grow by leaps and bounds."

"Now you are on the right track and prosperity and happiness is waiting for you," said Vikas. "I hope you are not bored."

"We had a wonderful discussion," said John. "I feel immensely motivated and delighted."

"Decide today that you are going to wake up cheerfully daily and start your day infused with passion. Reclaim the joy you had when you started your business. Do not do the things because you have to do, but, because you love them. Whatever mundane job you do, do it with enthusiasm and energy. Make constant never ending improvements in all the fields. There is always a room for improvement." articulated Vikas reassuringly with a smile. "Remember, what lies inside you, is more important than what lies behind you and in front of you. You are a unique creation of God and world is incomplete without you."

"One of your passions, you noted down on your passion card, is to visit your cherished destinations with your family members," Vikas reminded john. "Tell me, how many places you have visited so far, in India and abroad?"

"Only a few," John mumbled. "I rarely get time to visit them. Life is so busy."

"Is your passion not your life? Set priorities according to your vision and missions. In future, refer to your passion card time to time and live your life accordingly. You may, however, revise your passion card, time to time, in conformity with the changed scenario. Know your chief aim and subsidiary aims. Fulfill your passions. Life is short and it is too important to be wasted on trifles."

"Thanks Vikas, said John. "I feel immensely motivated."

"How many times you avail well deserved rest?" asked Vikas further. "Always take rest, whenever you feel like taking. Have you ever thought of modernization of your business?"

"No," John muttered. "I never thought on these lines."

"Do it now," said Vikas. "Why did you not try new areas of business?" asked Vikas. "Do you have some other business in your mind, which will give you satisfaction and which is also in conformity with your passions?"

"Yes," said John. "I have one more new business in my mind."

"That is excellent, try that. Venture and invest in such a new field," said Vikas. "If you do not change the way you work, and if you do not work for growth, the monotony will creep in and life will become cloudy and dull. Irving Wallace used to say: *'Every man can transform the world from one of monotony and drabness to one of excitement and adventure.'* Doing the same thing daily can be dull, monotonous and depressing; therefore, to get out of it, you need, temporarily, to change your routine."

"Now I can understand what change is needed," said Vikas.

"You can take a day off or change the way you are doing the things. One of the best ways to change the way you feel is to change your environment," Vikas reiterated.

"Do something new daily. Develop a new hobby or do something you have never tried before. This break will make you happier and more productive in life."

"Okay."

"There must, therefore, be some change and variation in your daily routine. It is a natural human tendency to get bored of doing a thing over and over again," said Vikas. "Daily routine, no matter how good it is, becomes dull with time. Too much of even a good thing is not that good. Even if you smile continuously, it is not delighting for you. One should be moderate in all the aspects of life."

"I feel that I am lacking something in my personality also," said John. "I have to readjust my attitude towards life."

"Invest in your personal growth, as you are doing now. You should invest in giving technical training to your employees to sharpen their tools," Vikas expatiated. "Then they can handle your business more efficiently and you can delegate your work to them safely to keep your mind free for better utilization."

"Very good suggestion, indeed," said John. "Motivational workshops for employees will also be useful."

"Yes John, such workshops for your employees will create an amiable environment in the work place and infuse enthusiasm in them to perform better voluntarily," Vikas suggested. "We organize such corporate workshops also."

"I will be glad, if you please spare some time for a workshop for my employees," John requested Vikas.

"Okay, we will discuss," said Vikas, "and I will let you know the probable dates for the workshop."

Chapter-17

Vikas is a basically happy person. He has got his own peculiar style of living life. He believes in slowing down to the speed of life and living life joyfully with an effortless ease. He also believes in making constant never ending improvements in all the fields, and at the same time, lives a blissful life. In the morning also, he is never in hurry. He, not only, usually gets up early in the morning, but also enjoys surfacing into each day slowly, with grace ease and lightness.

He had a wonderful sleep and woke up today also, as usual, quite early in the morning. There was only an imperceptibly faint light, filtering through the window slits. He knew by these signs that it was very early and that he could timely start the day.

He got up, smiled and stretched joyously. He poured some warm water in a glass and added fresh lime juice. Sipping slowly and mindfully, he visualized an extraordinary day ahead, conducting workshop with lot of interactions and interesting psychological games and exercises. He performed deep relaxing meditation for some time and set intention of the day.

There was a gentle rap on the door. He opened the door and found that Reena was standing smiling with arms spread. She hugged him and he responded with angel hug.

"You are looking fresh and gorgeous." Remarked Vikas.

"Thanks," chimed in Reena jubilantly. "You are also looking awesome."

"What were you doing, by the way? I hope, I have not come at improper time," Reena chuckled.

"No, you have arrived at proper time; proper, because now we will sip our morning tea together. But you have to wait for some time, till I set intention of the day," mumbled Vikas with a smile.

"Wow! It is a marvelous way to start the day," said Reena. "You require lot of time start the day this way."

"No, we do not require much time to set intentions of the day, for it is intensity, not the duration, that counts," Vikas articulated. "Also, setting intention is not waste of time. It is, on the other hand, an important way to start the day, planning and visualizing the glorious day ahead. Our destiny is shaped by our intentions. Intention is the starting point of every dream. It is the creative power that fulfills all of our needs, whether for abundance or spiritual awakening."

"Okay, go ahead, do it and guide me too, while doing it yourself. I am also eager to learn," said Reena with a charming smile. Her eyes lit up with curiosity.

He began by asking her to sit on a mat. She followed his voice as he instructed, "Close your eyes and do relaxing meditation for a few minutes… till your senses start responding more efficiently… While inhaling… breathe in unconditional love… joy… peace and abundance… Breathe out all stress… tension… worries… fear and resentment… Relax every part of your body… one by one," Vikas explained and demonstrated while doing it.

Reena followed the instructions and did what she was told.

"Do not force yourself… Take it easy…," further explained Vikas. "Be grateful to God for all the abundance and multitude of blessings, which surround you this very moment… The result of trying too hard, can never come even half way, as is achieved by doing things naturally, with an effortless ease."

She listened with focused mind and nodded to indicate 'yes'.

"We, sometimes have tough times, do not we?"

"Even in tough times, we are lucky to have something in our lives to be grateful for. Thank God for having so many amenities to make life a wonderful experience. Just look around; you will see so many things and the limitless universe to be grateful for. It is abundant and strangely accommodating. You should be grateful to God not only for having physical things, but for creating an invisible energy force or field of infinite possibilities around you," explained Vikas in detail. "You should have a firm belief in Him and in His powers. Your belief can impact the field of prospects and you can draw from it according to your passions and beliefs. Your belief will make connection to the Almighty, who will provide accurate and unlimited guidance."

"Okay."

"Bless everything, everybody and every situations in your life that you are grateful for," Vikas further elucidated in detail. "Forgive yourself and then forgive others. Now take a few more deep relaxing breaths to reflect on the things you would like to be forgiven for. Forgive yourself totally. Pray for the people who had wronged you and forgive them. Make sure that you, no longer, hold grudges against them."

She listened with full concentration.

"You are never alone and God is always there to help and guide you. You need His help, because you cannot solve problems alone. Take a few more breaths and decide what magnificent work you are going to do today and what type of help you require," said Vikas. "Release your intentions into the productive ground of pure potentiality. Visualize a rocking day ahead, thanking God in advance for numerous unfolding joys of the day ahead."

"It is a magnificent start of the day for me. I am so blissful. You made my day. Thank you Vikas," squeaked Reena, pouring tea with a charming smile, looking at him with love. "I wish, I could start my remaining mornings of my life setting intentions with you as I did today."

"I also liked it with you. Thank you, Reena," said Vikas with a smile.

"Please allow me to take your leave now, Vikas," said Reena, spreading her arms. She hugged Vikas again and walked out slowly, closing door behind.

He stepped out for a morning walk, almost immediately, as she left. The air was fresh and rejuvenating. The sky was clear and the eastern horizon was radiant with rosy shades and cold breeze was rustling the leaves and brushing his cheeks. The birds were no more silent by now. The unswerving chirping of birds was euphonic. Subsequently, he enjoyed swimming in the pool where other participants had also flocked. He also basked in the heat of steam and sauna rooms.

Today was the final day of the workshop. Vikas was happy that he could successfully accomplish his mission of organizing an exquisite workshop in an exotic island. The days flowed by swiftly, gliding by one after the other, wonderfully like the beads of a rosary, soon growing into a week. All the days were diversified, like distinct bands of a brilliant rainbow; full of vibrant colors, diversity and rejuvenation. All the days in the resort brought with them something fascinating, evocative and innovative.

Everybody was delighted and satisfied with their unforgettable stay on this island. The hotel staff was busy making the preparations for the closing and the certificate ceremony. The hall was elegantly decorated. A few media persons were also present to cover the closing ceremony on the last day of the workshop.

In the corner of the hall a few books and CDs were displayed. All including the hotel staff were flipping through the books.

"You may all see the books, but there is no need for participants to purchase the same, as everyone will get one set free along with pen drive containing the workshop material," said Vikas. "You may, however, purchase extra copies, if you want to gift the same to your friends."

"Time to time, we too organize such workshops here. You may give us a few copies for display," suggested Sofia. "If the copies are sold, the sale proceeds will be sent to you."

"Yes, I will give you the same," said Vikas.

"You are a magnificent creation of God with unlimited possibilities and unfathomable potential. This world is incomplete without you. This is time to manifest your best. You, very well know how magnificent a bud of a flower looks. It looks incredible, delicate, and exceptional. It is not aware of the splendor within, which it is going to manifest. It is also oblivious of the fact that its presence is going to add to the grandeur of the magnificent creation. You are all going to beautify the world," started Vikas with pleasant demeanor.

"I congratulate you all for successfully completing the course. We have interacted a lot and have enriched each other tremendously. We are now better equipped with magnificent ideas. We should put these ideas into practice, in our day-to-day lives and transplant these ideas into others minds also, by teaching them and helping them practice these ideas. Without practice ideas have no meaning."

Everybody listened him speak with interest and undivided attention. Media persons were also covering the proceedings of the closing ceremony.

"I hope, you all had a memorable stay here and enjoyed. I will be glad, if you share a few of your experiences and aha moments," added Vikas. He nodded at John who was eager to say something.

John stood up, came to the podium and said, "Good morning, ladies and gentlemen. I am happy I decided to attend this workshop. I had a wonderful stay here and learned a lot about living life in a magnificent manner. This workshop has transformed my life for better. It has changed my attitude to a considerable extent. Attitude makes lot of difference, especially when the attitude is positive. I have started looking at life from an entirely different angle with different attitude. I liked the way, the workshop was conducted. There were so many meaningful interactions. Also, there were practical exercises and psychological games galore. I will never forget beautiful moments spent here."

"Very good Mr. John, interjected Vikas. "Do you want to share some exceptional experience?"

"Yes. One day I got up in the morning, hearing a gentle rap on the door. There was a room service lady who brought tea and poured it for me. She noticed a paper slip near the door. She picked up the slip which had a remark, *'Do some random act of kindness or do something, at the first opportunity, which will make someone happy?'* She read the slip and handed over to me with a smile," said John. "I got up, read the slip and hugged the room service lady. First, she was taken a back, but soon she regained her composure and burst into laughing when I pointed at the slip."

Everybody laughed joyfully. Vinod raised his hand to share his views. He said, "It was a lovely experience of my life to visit this place and attend the workshop. This was a beautiful break from a busy schedule of my life. It was relaxing and this workshop changed my attitude towards life. Interaction among the participants was also magnificent."

Then he looked lovingly at Dr. Meena who was also looking at him with fond eyes and added, "I got opportunity to meet and interact with you all. Dr. Meena is now a very good friend of mine and we have decided to get married. I will invite you all to bless the occasion very soon."

He gesticulated at Dr. Meena. She readily came to the dais and both hugged each other. There was fervent clapping in the hall and huge smiles spread across everybody's face.

Sofia also offered to say a few words. She stood at her seat and said, "It was an amazing experience to attend this workshop. I am thankful to my General Manager who was kind enough to allow both of us to participate in this lovely workshop. This workshop has changed my attitude, to enable me to live a better life. I could understand what unconditional love is and now I am looking at life from a different angle. I got an opportunity to interact a lot, practice a lot and learn from each other. I could eliminate numerous fears and doubts and I am in position to take bolder decisions. I know how to 'love unconditionally and live joyfully'."

"Reena, you appear to be eager to say something," said Vikas, gesticulating at her.

"I never imagined that I would gain so much. I am, really, very happy, I attended this workshop. The stay in this exquisite island was very interesting lifetime experience. I shall always remember the beautiful moments shared with you. Thank you very much," said Reena. "Mr. Vikas, you are doing a great service to humanity to help them live a wonderful life. I have become your fan."

"Only fan?" remarked Mitali, smiling brightly. "Or…"

"Yes, for now" said Reena smiling. "You never know… I am a tough minded optimist."

Vikas called names of all the participants, one by one, and they came to collect their certificates. Everybody clapped fervently and joyfully.

All of you are requested to please come, we will have a light refreshment outside in the lawn. Everybody was in a jubilant mood. There were many colorful lanterns in the lawn with candles in them.

"Everybody, please light candles and write your wishes on the lantern covers with a marker and release them to let them fly in the sky. Release your wishes and let the universe arrange to fulfill them for you," said Vikas with a smile.

Everybody enjoyed seeing colorful lanterns flying in the sky.

"Let us plant trees, in memory of our visit to this beautiful island resort. We will visit this place again, someday later, to see how splendidly they have grown."

"Everybody, please write letters to yourself, in which you write what you have resolved today. These letters will be posted to you 6 months from now. These letters will showcase your emotions."

Printed in the United States
By Bookmasters